DOCTOR
JACK
and Other Tales

DOCTOR
JACK
and Other Tales

THE ADVENTURES OF VIOLA STEWART
JOURNAL #1

KAREN J CARLISLE

Kraken Publishing

Doctor Jack and Other Tales
The Adventures of Viola Stewart Journal #1

A catalogue record for this book is available from the National Library of Australia

Also available separately as eBooks.

This book is written in British English.
Printed in Australia.
First Edition 2015
Second Edition 2016
Third Edition 2022

Typeset in Times Roman 10pt.

Published by Kraken Publishing.
www.krakenpublishing.com

To my family and friends who supported me in my darkest hours.

Contents

Three Short Stories

Novella

Bonus Excerpt

Three Short Stories

The Day of the Dirigible

Today Viola was on her way to watch the landing of the first steam flight from Europe!

She squeaked with delight as she played with the levers on a wooden control box. Her mini-dirigible bobbed amongst the passengers of the four o'clock train, its pink bunting tickling the face of the conductor.

Viola grinned. She had always dreamed of flying away in her own steam-powered airship.

She snatched her toy from the air, and pushed a button on the teacup sized gondola. Small puffs of steam expelled from the base, as the miniature frilled balloon slowly ascended and set off on another tour of the carriage.

Her father glanced up from his newspaper.

"Be careful, Viola," he said. He flipped the page and returned to the afternoon news.

A flick of a toggle; steam now trickled from one side, manoeuvring the airship parallel to the carriage windows, as it chugged along the aisle.

A tall, dark gentleman swatted at her toy airship. The pleated frill on its metal gondola brushed along his grey bowler hat, nudging it askew. He grumbled as the pink confection floated harmlessly away, followed by a giggling Viola with bobbing ringlets.

The man in the grey bowler hat surveyed the dirigible, as it continued on its voyage of vexation, especially attentive of the small box that controlled it. Most passengers ignored the toy, not even giving Viola a second glance. He smiled and adjusted his grey cravat.

The weather had been fortunate. The skies were clear, with little cloud cover, ensuring a large turnout befitting such a momentous occasion. The spectators were corralled behind a fence, controlling access to the landing field. Women jiggled their large skirts, as they twirled their way through the ever-swelling crowd.

Viola clutched her precious toy dirigible, as her father ushered her towards the front of the throng. She watched eagerly as carriages arrived depositing their passengers at the VIP seating. A continuous line of men and women in fancy clothes, and with snooty visages, emerged from the well-appointed cabs. Each seemed more interested in the occupants of the Royal Box than the impending pageant. Not one looked skyward in anticipation.

Viola quickly tired watching the earth-bound transportation. She tugged on her father's trouser leg.

"Go play with your dirigible," he said. "I will fetch you when the airship arrives."

Viola flicked a switch on her dirigible. She blew gently at the small puffs of steam that emerged, and traced the swirling eddies as they trailed the floating concoction of lace and ribbons. The dirigible ascended above the crowd, then dipped low. A woman squealed as the dirigible tapped her ornately trimmed bonnet, before continuing on its adventure.

Viola flipped another toggle on the control box. Steam trickled from one side, redirecting the airship straight into the arms of the gentleman with the grey bowler and cravat.

He flashed a shiny badge on his matching waistcoat.

"I will have to confiscate this, Miss," he said.

Viola saw his shiny badge, bowed her head and surrendered the control box.

The man melted back into the crowd.

Gone was her beloved pink, frilly dirigible.

The Man in Grey had followed his quarry from the train. Now that it was in his possession, he would not relinquish it. It would serve well. He retrieved a compact brown-papered package from his coat pocket and placed it in the metal gondola.

A faint smell of sulphur and saltpetre wafted upwards as a tiny coiled contraption pierced the packaging. A turn of the small key and the coil began to unwind, edging a small hammer closer to a blasting cap - enough spark required to catch the black powder.

The control box was easy to master and the dirigible was airborne again.

All eyes were now on the arriving airship, savouring the historical importance of the event. Only Viola was distracted by her miniature pink-trimmed balloon, with its heavily-laden gondola, nudging closer to the airship.

The jubilant onlookers cheered as the landing lines dropped, followed by the dumping of water ballast.

The pink bunting scraped along the airship's helium filled envelope.

"My dirigible!"

Viola's cries went unheard above the cheering crowd - as did the tink of the coil as it released and the clap of the hammer as it hit the blasting cap.

No one heard the sizzle as the black powder flared into life. The flames tickled the linen envelope, its lacquer-coating promptly giving in to its caress.

The rear of the airship settled. Too early. A tense hush took over the jubilant crowd, as a second ballast was dumped. The spray sent mechanics running for cover and drenched the occupants of the Royal Box.

The flames ignited the hydrogen with a whoosh.

A collective gasp rippled through the onlookers.

The balloon shuddered as the escaping gas exploded.

It took less than thirty seconds for the airship to crumple before them. The leading edge blazed with a rim of brilliant orange, consuming the envelope as it raced forward. The balloon's skeleton glowed for only a second, followed by its cascading collapse. The remains of the airship fell to the ground before the stunned witnesses.

The crowd surged forward to aid in the disaster.

One carriage departed, a man in a grey cravat its only passenger.

Viola wailed for the loss of her dirigible.

In the chaos of billowing black smoke and sizzling water, one of the technicians tripped over a small metal object. Pink bows were barely visible under the soot and scorches on the twisted miniature gondola.

THE END

An Eye for Detail

Viola opened the window shutter, allowing the light to enter. It slowly danced across the room, chasing away the dark. She waited for her eyes to adapt to the change, drinking in the sun's warmth on her skin.

The playful squeals of children drifted up from the street. Happy sounds. Soothing sounds. For Viola, they also brought sorrow. It was doubtful that she would have children now. Her plans changed abruptly following her husband's death more than a year ago.

Viola looked down to the street, hoping to see the source of the children's excitement. A red-headed man in a grey suit and bowler hat passed out apples. The children snatched them eagerly.

"Gutter-snipes!" declared a woman's voice behind her. "I am so sorry you have to deal with them, Doctor Stewart."

Viola turned away from the window. A well-dressed middle aged woman sat in the large chair at the other side of the room. She was dressed smartly, in magenta silk and velvet, with an astonishing array of passmenterie for an afternoon dress. Her fashionable bustle was wedged between the arms of the chair, forcing her to balance precariously on its edge. This amused Viola, lifting her from her melancholy and necessitating a deft movement of her hand to hide her smile.

Both the woman and her magnificent, voluminous skirts appeared small in comparison to the sparsely furnished room. Aside from the chair, the room boasted only a tall wooden stool cushioned in leather, a reasonably sized desk covered with assorted instruments and cases, a bookshelf and a small locked cupboard.

To the side of the chair was a strange looking contraption. A large metal board faced the woman, shielding her from its workings on the opposite side - a brass cylinder and a small brass lamp with a long, thin glass chimney. Below the complicated rig was a table with a small spherical concave reflector pierced with a pinhole and a selection of glass lenses arrayed in a compact velvet lined box.

The woman shifted in the chair, adjusting her bustle for comfort. A pair of half-circle metal frames perched on her nose. Viola pointed towards the letter chart at the opposite side of the room, its letters now illuminated by the additional light provided by the open window.

"Is that better, Lady Calthorpe?" Viola enquired, as she crossed the room to stand by the chair.

Lady Calthorpe squinted slightly and nodded slowly. Viola reached out her hand and spun a metal-rimmed lens that lay in the frame.

"Ah yes, Doctor Stewart!" Lady Calthorpe smiled. "That is a great improvement."

Viola removed the frames, examined the lenses and wrote the numbers down in her notebook.

"I will send a note when they are ready, Lady Calthorpe, if that is acceptable to you."

"Yes, yes. That would be perfectly acceptable." Lady Calthorpe stood and straightened the wrinkles from her skirt. "I shall only wear them when absolutely required, of course."

Viola smiled. *Ladies and their vanity.*

"One day they will become fashionable, my Lady."

Lady Calthorpe shook her head.

"Only if they can make one's waist appear smaller, my dear." A polite smile flickered over her lips. "Good day, Doctor Stewart."

She retrieved her bonnet, taking advantage of the wall mirror by the door, to ensure not to disturb her fastidiously plaited coiffure with her hat pin. She examined her reflection, sighed and carefully re-arranged a wayward lock of hair.

Viola waited until she heard Lady Calthorpe leave the front room, before she leaned through the doorway.

"Was that the last for the day, Miss Blake?" she asked.

Miss Blake finished writing in a large book and looked up. She was a short, young woman in a sensible dress of blue linen. Her hair was blonde, set in a practical fashion.

"Yes, Doctor Stewart." Miss Blake closed the book and stood, straightening her skirts. "Tea?"

Viola nodded.

Viola was usually confronted by the street children when she returned from her late afternoon walk. Today, all was quiet outside the townhouse; she missed the children's rambunctious diversions that heralded her arrival home.

A lone girl with long blonde braids, sat on the step. Viola recognised the girl; she had often seen her playing in the street. The girl looked up at Viola with tear filled eyes.

"What happened, Lucy?" Viola asked.

"It's Elly," Lucy replied, wiping the tears away. "The grey man took her away."

Though Viola had no children of her own, her maternal instincts were already in full flight.

What men? What happened?

Lucy sniffed and wiped her eyes but was distracted by the sound of a crowd gathering at the entrance to the nearby alley, before Viola could ask her any questions. Viola reached into her pockets, retrieved a small plump orange and handed it to the young girl.

"Don't worry Lucy," she replied.

Viola pulled her gloves up, straightened her skirts and joined the crowd.

The body of a small girl lay in the unlit alley, partially obscured by one of the Constables who were in attendance. Viola moved closer. A hessian bag partially covered her head. Viola's heart skipped. It was Elly! A second Constable ventured to the edge of the crowd, asking for possible witnesses or anyone who may have known the girl. He glanced over the crowd, shrugged his shoulders and returned to his partner.

"Must be a street orphan," he whispered to the first Constable.

"Better remove the body then. Nothing more to learn here."

Little Elly's body was quickly covered and, as it was carried past, Viola caught a familiar sweet aroma. She knew the smell from her late husband's surgery. It was the unmistakable odour of chloroform.

The spectators began to crowd the area where Elly had lain. Viola heard the faint tinkling noise of glass over stones. Turning her head towards the noise, she saw a faint glint of light beyond the main crowd. She snatched up the find and slipped it into her pocket. There was no privacy, and too little light, to examine it here.

She returned to Greater Marylebone Street to examine the trinket under the street lamp. The item was instantly recognisable, even under the soft gas lighting. She worked with them daily - a small convex lens, similar to those in her instrument case, used to view the retina of the eye. There was a dusting of black powder on one edge.

Curious.

It obviously did not belong to the child. There were no other oculists in the immediate area and it was not part of her equipment; everything had been accounted for earlier that day.

Curiouser.

Viola surmised that there was a high possibility that it must have belonged to the murderer.

She glanced back into the alley. The Constables had already left to return the child's body to the station. She wrapped the lens in her lace handkerchief and placed it in her pocket for safekeeping until morning.

I will visit my dear friend, Doctor Collins, tomorrow. He may find this interesting.

The next morning was overcast and brought with it a continuous drizzle of rain, necessitating the ordering of a cab to travel to Marylebone Police Station. Viola was disappointed. She loved long walks.

Miss Blake had rearranged her appointments; giving Viola plenty of time to visit Doctor Collins at the Marylebone Police Station. He preferred to conduct Police business in the mornings as his skills were usually required in the afternoons for his practice on Harley Street. This suited Viola's afternoon appointment schedule; Upper class women rarely emerged before luncheon.

Viola was greeted by an unfamiliar, fresh faced Constable at the Division Station.

"Good morning Constable," she said. "I have some information with respect to last night's murder off Greater Marylebone Street."

"No need, ma'am. All is in hand. You can return to your family," The Constable did not even bother to look up from his paperwork.

"Pardon?" Viola pursed her lips.

Fortunately for the young Constable, Doctor Collins emerged from the office door into the waiting room. He nodded and flashed a smile in Viola's direction. Doctor Collins was tall and dark, with piercing blue eyes and had a habit of neatening his fashionably wax tipped moustache.

The Constable looked blankly at Viola, seemingly oblivious to his blunder.

"And one wonders how the Metropolitan gets its reputation." Viola gritted her teeth.

The Constable fidgeted with his watch chain.

I'll teach him some manners.

Doctor Collins glanced in Viola's direction. He bit his lip and stepped between them.

"Constable Jones, may I present Doctor Viola Stewart of Greater Marylebone Street."

It was not the first time he had rescued an unsuspecting Constable, Viola thought.

Constable Jones nodded in reply. There was nothing like formalities to bring order and manners back to any situation and Constable Jones appeared to be in great need of manners.

Introductions complete, Viola followed Doctor Collins into the examination room.

She noted the small size of the body on the table and frowned.

"Her name was Elly. She was an orphan. She played in front of my house," said Viola. She took a slow breath and busied herself straightening the necropsy equipment, careful not to let her friend see the tear in her eye.

Doctor Collins removed the coverings to reveal the girl's pale face. It had been a pretty face, in life. Now the left eye was pulled partially out of the socket. Viola had a strange feeling there was something familiar about it; something she could not quite remember.

"I have another one like her," Doctor Collins said calmly.

Viola took a sharp breath.

"Two days ago. Another orphan," he continued. "The eyes were intact but the face was covered by a similar hessian bag and there was the smell of..."

"Chloroform!" Viola spun to face the doctor and nodded. "I smelled it too." Viola was reminded of the reason for her visit. She pulled the handkerchief from her pocket, revealing the small lens and handed it to the doctor.

"I found this, not far from her body. The Constables did not bother to search the area." She held it closer to the gas lamp. "Look, there is a black substance on the edge."

The two doctors exchanged glances, sighed and began to examine the deposit on the lens.

Viola stood at the window. She looked down to the street. It had been unusually quiet for the past two days. As she closed the shutter, she saw a red-headed man playing cricket with the boys. Lucy sat alone, playing a game of Knuckle-bones.

Poor Lucy. Viola's heart ached. She had been about Lucy's age, when she lost her own sister. They had been peas in a pod - like Lucy and Elly.

Viola secured the shutter, wishing it could close off the world as easily as it shut out the light.

She returned to her patient and moved the stool as close as she could, considering both were wearing corsets, bustles and several layers of frilled skirts. Her patient's pupils were large and dark.

The atropine has done its work well.

"Now, let me look at these eyes, Mrs Cogswell. You say the flashing lights started a few days ago?"

Mrs Cogswell nodded. Viola turned up the small brass lamp on the opposite side of the metal board, just to the left of her chair. Mrs Cogswell winced. Her pupils remained fixed and dilated.

Perhaps too well. Viola apologised and dimmed the light slightly.

She raised one of the lenses in her left hand, and moved it slightly to focus while she peered through the hole of her ophthalmoscope. Before long she could see the blood vessels at the back of the eye. All seemed clear, until the lens clouded over unexpectedly. Viola thought she had seen the blurry, grey figure of a man in place of the vessels. She flinched, dropping the lens to the floor. Mrs Cogswell gasped and shielded her eyes, as the room flooded with light.

"I am sorry Doctor Stewart, Mrs Cogswell. Doctor Collins said it was urgent Police business." Miss Blake swooped into the room, retrieved the lens, which had rolled under the desk, and placed it on the bookshelf.

Viola turned to see Doctor Collins standing in the doorway. His grey plaid suit was perfectly tailored to fit his tall frame. He held a matching bowler in his hands. His gaze flickered in the direction of Viola's patient. His smile faded. He quickly apologised and closed the door.

"I am sorry for the interruption Mrs Cogswell," said Viola.

She twisted on her stool and turned off the small brass lantern. She gently pried Mrs Cogswell's eyelids open and studied her patient. "The good news is that there appears to be no damage."

"Thank goodness," replied Mrs Cogswell.

Viola led Mrs Cogswell to the door, arranging a veil over her face to reduce the light's intensity.

"Miss Blake will attend you. If you have any other problems, please contact me."

Doctor Collins bowed his head and apologised to Mrs Cogswell, as he entered the examination room and closed the door behind her.

"I must apologise for the intrusion at such a late hour, and without an appointment, but I was sure you would want to hear the information now in my possession." He awaited a reply.

Viola was distracted, lost in her own thoughts. She retrieved the loose lens, from the bookshelf, and replaced it in its case.

"The substance on the lens was indeed silver oxide which is used in making photographic plates. The Constables are checking on photographers in the area," Doctor Collins continued. He approached Viola and placed a gentle hand on her shoulder.

"Is there something wrong?" he asked.

Viola turned, wide-eyed with terror, barely able to catch her breath. Doctor Collins dropped his hand immediately, and apologised for such intimacy. Viola shook her head.

"No, you don't understand," she replied. "I know why he is covering the head and removing the eyes!"

Viola recounted the incident with his reflection in the lens. It had reminded her of something she had heard as a child. A superstition; in cases of violent death, the last images were fixed permanently to the retina of the eye. Recent scientific papers had reported the German physiologist, Kühne, had done experiments on *optograms* in an effort to prove the theory.

"He does not want to be identified." Viola looked Doctor Collins in the eye. "There was a man in a grey suit. Lucy said she saw a Man in Grey take Elly. She *saw* him!"

Viola's eyes widened. A cold shiver ran down her spine.

"Henry," she whispered. "There was a Man in Grey with the children, just now."

Viola rushed through the door and into the street, followed by Doctor Collins. A lone boy dragged his cricket bat along the cobblestones.

"The man in the grey suit," Doctor Collins demanded. "Where is he?"

Viola scanned the street. *Empty.*

"And where is Lucy?" Viola's boot kicked something on the ground, sending it skittering into the gutter. *One of Lucy's knuckle-bones.*

"Where is she?" Viola insisted.

The boy pointed towards High Street. Doctor Collins flipped the boy a shiny penny to inform the Marylebone Station Constabulary of the unfolding events.

Reliable, as always.

Viola hitched up her petticoats and sped towards High Street as fast as her skirts would allow. Doctor Collins followed in her wake.

Viola raced down High Street. Early evening shadows were already being cast by the rooftops.

Which way to turn?

Her heart raced. She spied one of Lucy's knuckle-bones on the ground.

Clever girl.

She smiled and headed south. A few more knuckle-bones led her into Cross Keys Close via Marylebone Lane, further away from the street lighting and deeper into the growing gloom. Viola found herself at the end of the Close, with no lamplight to guide her. She slowed, letting her eyes adapt to the increasing shadows. Her foot knocked against something.

Viola crouched down. She could make out the outline of a small girl. Both eyes were missing.

Too late.

As Doctor Collins turned the corner, he could see no sign of Viola. He paced a few steps in either direction, crushing a knuckle-bone underfoot. He remembered seeing some near Doctor Stewart's rooms. He headed south in search of more breadcrumbs.

Viola fought back the tears. She could still smell the chloroform used. The smell was growing stronger.

My imagination is playing tricks on me.

Viola stood and turned to see a red-headed man in a grey suit.

Darkness descended.

Slowly the light began to return as the haze that encompassed Viola's head dissolved. Her vision slowly cleared, along with her thoughts. She had a ghastly headache, unlike any she had felt before. She took a shallow breath. There was still a faint sweet smell. In the fuzzy distance of the darkened room, a figure wiped his hands, placed the cloth into a basket, pulled down his sleeves and walked closer.

Viola sat upright. Her torso muscles strained under her weight. She gasped. She no longer wore a corset nor bustle.

Viola flailed at the table beside her, searching for a weapon as she eyed the approaching figure. Her fingers knocked a kidney dish and wrapped themselves around the scalpel she found there.

The figure came into focus. Viola found herself staring into the most piercing blue eyes she had ever seen.

"You won't be needing that." Doctor Collins' voice was soft.

Viola dropped the scalpel, missing the kidney dish.

"Lucy?" she asked fearfully.

Doctor Collins shook his head.

"We only just found you in time."

Viola tried to focus on her friend. She still had problems accommodating and judging distances. Her eyes ached.

Obviously I am still recovering from the chloroform. A slight dizzy spell necessitated her holding her head where she felt bandages covering her eye.

"Viola," Doctor Collins said calmly. "I have something to tell you."

THE END

The Magic Lantern

This will be a magnificent portrait," said Brewer. "Don't move." He flipped the black cloth over his head.

Lord and Lady Hearst each took a breath and sat motionless. There was a blinding flash, quickly followed by cursing. Thick acrid smoke surrounded them. Slowly it rose and wafted through the open window revealing now empty chairs. The smell of sulphur lingered.

"Well done, Brewer." Mr Kirby slapped the photographer on the back. Brewer slipped out from under the large camera cloth, trying not to breathe in the fumes. His assistant, George, scurried forward to retrieve any remaining paraphernalia belonging to the chairs' recent occupants, coughing as he did so.

Mr Kirby moved closer to the camera, Brewer deftly slipped the black cloth over the camera box, obscuring it from Kirby's enquiring eyes. George smiled as he watched Mr Kirby frown in frustration.

"You know the arrangements." Brewer held the cloth securely.

"Five hundred pounds." Mr Kirby beamed.

Brewer shook his head. "Not enough I am afraid."

Kirby's frown returned. He fetched his hat and cane, nodding in the direction of the two men and their illusive contraption. "I shall speak to my employer." He huffed, spun on his heel and left.

"Are you satisfied, Mr Grey?" asked Brewer.

A small man in a well-cut grey suit and matching bowler hat emerged from the shadows. Mr Grey represented a society as secretive as they were affluent. Brewer did not care why they were interested in his experiments, only that they offered more funding.

"I think we may have a deal, Mr Brewer. One thousand guineas and ongoing fees for further research," said Mr Grey. "We will formalise the contract once I have witnessed the last part of the demonstration." He tipped his hat and excused himself.

"George, I think we have found permanent employment." Brewer said. He smiled, placed a hand on his beloved machine and patted it gently.

Doctor Collins sat opposite Viola in the carriage. She looked resplendent in a pale violet bustle dress. He noted the subtle rosettes that followed the line of the bodice toward her décolletage. Gone were the austerity and dark colours of full mourning. He was glad. The colour was stunning on her. He smiled. Viola was prepared to re-enter society. She deserved a little cheer.

"I have never seen a magic lantern show," said Viola.

Doctor Collins watched as her eye sparkled in excitement. She tugged at her dark curls self-consciously, allowing the fringe to fall over the small pale eye patch that covered her right eye. It was a terrible reminder of a past adventure and memories best forgotten.

Dr Collins caught her hand gently and placed it in her lap.

"Don't fuss, Viola." His hand lingered a little longer on hers.

With a jolt, the carriage halted. Viola lurched forward in her seat, closer to her friend. He caught her around the waist, preventing her from falling further.

Viola blushed.

"We've arrived."

The hall was crammed with excited patrons. The two doctors made their way past some of the more colourful locals to find their seats.

"Lady Calthorpe is attending with Lady Hearst tonight. She does want to meet you," said Viola.

Doctor Collins chuckled.

"In case she suffers from the vapours, no doubt."

Viola raised her hand to her mouth to hide her smile. She did enjoy his candid sense of humour. She searched the sea of top hats, elaborate bonnets and coiffures for Lady Hearst and her husband and spied the unmistakable bonnet of Lady Calthorpe in the row in front of them. Two seats remained vacant next to her. The Hearsts had not arrived.

The clock chimed half past seven. Slowly the hall lights dimmed. Viola recognised several patients and local gentry. Lady Calthorpe glanced at those around her, rummaged through her reticule and perched her spectacles on the end of her nose.

In the dark the wide-eyed crowd hushed and leaned forward, all eyes fixed on the screen. A small point of light appeared before them, slowly growing into a circle that flickered like a ring of fire of a most radiant red hue. The ring metamorphosed into a star, its tips becoming a brilliant blue then erupting into a kaleidoscope of geometric patterns within. The audience gasped. Such a riot of colour!

The myriad of colours dissolved into a painting of a jester; his legs rocked from side to side as he danced. The crowd laughed and cheered as they were entertained by a further series of animated pictures.

Doctor Collins clapped heartily. "Amazing!"

"It is a clever illusion."

Viola smiled. *Optics was never his strong point.*

Doctor Collins turned to her, his attention distracted.

"The projectionist moves the slides fast enough that the eye cannot see the gaps between slides so it appears the jester is dancing," she explained.

Next, a deep voice narrated the story of *Alice in Wonderland* accompanied by more of the magical illusions. A blue caterpillar, atop a gigantic mushroom, elongated before their very eyes. Puffs of smoke filled the air around them, re-enforcing the illusion.

"... or move a glass slide to create the illusion," continued Viola. She noted her companion's smile fading slightly, and added: "It is a skill to be sure."

The audience clapped as the story came to an end.

"And now for the latest wonder," announced the Master of Ceremonies. "Photographs that move. The French are working on the cinemascope but we have perfected them already - with the Magic Lantern." His hand lifted through the smoke and pointed at the screen.

Photos of urchins playing hopscotch showed girls jumping slowly forward then backwards again. Viola was impressed with the quality of movement, quite smooth and lifelike. The final photograph was a portrait of an upper class couple seated formally, at first, then jumping up in shock. Viola gasped quietly in recognition.

"Oh my, it is Lord and Lady Hearst." Viola searched the row in front of them. Their seats were still vacant. "What a pity they were not here to see it. They will be disappointed."

"Perhaps they were too embarrassed," said Dr Collins.

With the demonstration complete, Brewer removed the glass photo plate from the Magic Lantern and handed it to Mr Grey, who held it up towards the gas lamp light, squinting to view the image more clearly. As he watched, the composed couple suddenly jumped up in fright. The scene repeated itself.

"As you can see, our initial experiments in transferring light and energy into two dimensions have proven successful. However there are still some technical difficulties," said Brewer.

"Some natives avoid their photos being taken. They think that it steals their souls," said George as he smiled and polished the brass of the Magic Lantern.

"And does it, Mr Brewer?" Mr Grey diverted his attention towards Brewer and his ingenious invention.

Brewer and George exchanged glances. Mr Grey knew Brewer could not afford to lose such a lucrative contract and, with it, his dream of catching the attention of the scientific establishment of London. No wonder he was concerned.

"We have further investigations. Firstly, to confirm whether the photo plate is just a physical representation of the subjects. Secondly, to ascertain if the soul has also been captured intact."

Mr Grey smiled. Either way, he knew this was a valuable commodity. If the soul was lost, The Society's plan to transport spies over the borders would be defeated. However, if Brewer could revert the photographic images to their original form, The Society would have an almost foolproof method of transporting contraband and secrets though customs.

"Good work, Mr Brewer." Mr Grey slid the plate into a slot in a nearby box, alongside other photo plates. "How long is your projection to perfect the reversal?"

"Within the month. Our contract will provide the necessary capital to complete the apparatus for the final confirming experiments."

Mr Grey nodded.

"My superiors will be pleased." He removed his grey bowler, examined it carefully and flicked off some unseen lint before replacing it with a sound tap.

"We shall discuss this again very soon, Mr Brewer," he said.

Mr Brewer extended his hand towards his new benefactor. Mr Grey accepted the gesture, avoided George's handshake, and left the projection room.

The excited audience emerged from the Magic Lantern Show and spilled into the foyer. The air buzzed with chatter. Animated voices proclaimed the success of the fantastic spectacle they had just witnessed. Viola drank in the cheery atmosphere. It was an excellent way to mark the end of her bereavement. Doctor Collins grinned at Viola.

"You look pleased with yourself," she said.

"And you look happy," Doctor Collins replied. "So yes, I am pleased." He rocked on his heels and took a deep breath.

Lady Calthorpe fanned herself, as she slipped next to Viola.

"It is uncomfortably hot with such a crowd," she said, as she admired Viola's matching eye patch. "How vaudevillian of you." She snapped her fan shut and clapped her hands together. "I must have the name of your dressmaker. I shall have to purchase one at my earliest convenience."

Viola felt the heat in her cheeks.

"Ah, Lady Calthorpe, how are you this evening?" asked Doctor Collins, as he placed a gentle hand on Viola's arm.

Viola felt him guide her backwards, as he stepped forward, placing himself between her and Lady Calthorpe. *Perfect timing.*

"Thank you," she whispered.

He nodded slightly, not taking his gaze from Lady Calthorpe. "I was hoping to speak to Lord Hearst this evening. I do hope he and his wife are not unwell..."

Viola slipped through the crowd. *Where to hide?* She glanced around the foyer, sidestepping behind one of the foyer's large marble columns. She looked back toward Doctor Collins. He was still deep in conversation with Lady Calthorpe. He smiled and nodded, while his hands fidgeted unseen behind his back.

Viola leaned against the pillar, stretching her fingers out over its surface. The rock was cool and unyielding. She took a slow breath and let the chill run up her arms to cool her cheeks.

A flash of peripheral movement caught her attention. A small man in a grey suit, with matching bowler, entered the foyer from the projection room. He wiped his grey gloves on a crisp, white handkerchief as he crossed the foyer. He checked over his shoulder as he neared the side door. He placed his hand on the door knob and hesitated, glancing to each side before he exited.

Viola sighed and poured herself a second cup of tea. Lady Calthorpe fidgeted with her cake. Her tea was cold; not that she had noticed.

"It has been almost a week," Lady Calthorpe said. "I called on them for tea two days ago. They were not at home, and no word as to when they will return."

Viola nodded and drank her Darjeeling. Hot wisps tickled her nose, distracting her as her guest expressed concern, yet again. Viola's gaze wandered, her attention caught by a slip of white taffeta peeking past the precisely pressed pleating of Lady Calthorpe's hem. Viola sucked in her lip, as she hid behind the tea cup. Lady Calthorpe would be horrified at such disarray.

"Where could they be?" Lady Calthorpe shook her head, her bonnet wobbling precariously with the furiosity of her dismay. "Even their butler has no idea of ..."

A knock at the front door gave Viola a short reprieve. Lady Calthorpe stopped mid-sentence. She glanced wide-eyed at the door, and whisked off her spectacles. Muffled voices were followed by another knock on the parlour door.

A petite brunette in sensible service attire and white cap opened the door and bobbed.

"Doctor Collins for you, Miss," said Polly.

"Thank you Polly."

Doctor Collins strode into the parlour. His tall, lean figure cut a dashing silhouette as he approached them. He removed his hat, and bowed briefly in Lady Calthorpe's direction.

"Good morning, Doctor Collins," said Lady Calthorpe.

His clear blue eyes flicked in her direction but quickly returned to Viola.

"Doctor Stewart." His bow lingered.

"Do sit down, Doctor Collins," said Viola.

Doctor Collins clapped his hands and rubbed them together. "Ah, Polly. Do you have any of your fruitcake, or perhaps some of your glorious chocolate cake?"

Polly smiled and nodded.

"Lady Calthorpe was just telling me about the strange disappearance of Lord and Lady Hearst," said Viola. She peered at Doctor Collins over the rim of her teacup, glad to have someone to divert Her Ladyship's attention.

Doctor Collins winked at Viola and turned to face Lady Calthorpe.

"Pray tell me all the news, Lady Calthorpe. You must be at your wit's end," He listened to a fresh retelling of the situation, nodding when she took a breath, his only reprieve the fresh pot of tea and cake left on the tea tray by Polly.

Finally the hall clock chimed midday, distracting Viola's garrulous guest from her monologue.

"Please forgive me, I must dash," said Lady Calthorpe. "I have a luncheon engagement." She extracted her voluminous silk skirts from her chair, with great expertise, and excused herself.

Dr Collins chuckled, his eyes glinting with a hint of mischief.

"How does she manage to take so few breaths?" he said.

"Hush. You are no longer at University, Doctor Collins. Lady Calthorpe comes from a very distinguished family and is a very well-paying patient of mine."

He raised an eyebrow. Viola tapped his wrist. "What will I do with you?"

Viola took a long sip of calming tea. "But she did propose a conundrum, the whereabouts of Lord and Lady Hearst."

"The incident has been reported to the Constabulary. There are no leads," he replied.

"But there is!" Viola leaned towards the doctor and took his hand. "They had an appointment with the Magic Lantern Show's photographer on the day of their disappearance." She arched her left eyebrow and met his gaze directly with her remaining eye.

"I don't trust photographers," she said. The memory of her injury was still too raw.

Doctor Collins nodded.

"I am sure Constable Jones will be making enquiries."

Again the arched eyebrow.

"The Constabulary aren't the quickest with their enquiries, even when high society is involved," she replied. "So I will make an appointment for a sitting tomorrow."

"If your suspicions are valid, that could be dangerous, Viola." Deep furrows were now etched in his forehead.

Viola straightened her skirts as she retreated to a less intimate distance.

"I will make an appointment for a sitting," said Doctor Collins. "But I will inform you of everything of course, my dear." He offered her the last piece of cake. "Would you like more tea?"

Viola pulled her skirts in behind the shrubbery, and peered through the foliage. She watched as Doctor Collins was greeted at the door by a slightly dishevelled man with a poorly knotted neck tie.

"Doctor Collins. I have an appointment at ten," he said.

"Mr Brewer, your photographer." Brewer shook Doctor Collins' hand. He unrolled his sleeves and fumbled with his cuff links. "I must apologise. My assistant is running late."

Viola climbed up to the front window and stood outside on tiptoe, her hand clutching the edge of the sill. She watched Brewer usher the doctor into the front parlour. The centre of the room was dominated by an octagonal parquetry table on which several large display books lay. Brewer ushered the doctor towards one of the padded leather chairs and placed one of the large books before him.

With Brewer unwittingly occupied by Doctor Collins, Viola saw her opportunity. She made her way to the front door, only to find it still on the latch. She eased it open.

The muted conversation wafted toward Viola, as she slipped into the hallway and checked the closed door opposite the parlour. It was locked.

Bother.

Doctor Collins would scold her for following him. *He's being over protective.*

She huffed silently and straightened her shoulders. *It was my idea to investigate the photographer. Why should he have all the fun?*

Viola lifted her skirts and crept past the parlour door, and entered the photographer's studio. To the left, plush velvet drapes held back the daylight from entering through a large window, and concealed the room from prying eyes. To the right, a stream of light from a smaller window spilled over an oak desk.

Viola quickly scanned the desk. She sifted through its narrow drawers. She pulled out a leather-bound notebook and flipped through it. Each page was crammed with diagrams of lenses, ray diagrams and scrawled notes.

Wedged at the back of the drawer was a small, gilded, double-barrelled pistol. The handle was patterned with black enamel. The barrels were so short as to be almost non-existent. *Easily concealed.*

Viola peered down the barrels. *One bullet in each.* She reached into the folds of her skirt and slipped the pistol into the hidden pocket, followed by the notebook.

She turned to survey the rest of the studio. A movable curtain partially divided the room into two sections. Beyond the dividing curtain, to the left, stood a large mahogany box camera atop an adjustable wood base, its legs finished with metal wheels.

What a clever idea.

Beyond the camera stood a leather-upholstered chair. Behind the chair, at head height, was a clamp-like claw atop a metal stand. A system of ropes and pulleys suspended a voluminous draped cloth from the ceiling. Viola could not resist the temptation to tug gently at one of the knotted rope ends. The cloth above her twitched, opening to reveal an over-sized sky light. She winced as bright sunlight illuminated the chair and revealed a small wooden door, partially obscured by a painted backdrop, behind the chair.

Intrigued, Viola opened the door to reveal a store room. It was cramped in comparison to the studio, the size of a modest butler's pantry. Small boxes and optical paraphernalia packed the wall shelving. Most intriguing of all was a second camera, more complicated than the first and obviously more expensive. It was made of polished mahogany, and had two small ancillary lenses which sat above a main over-sized lens system. All three lenses were encased in etched brass tubes.

A pile of large photographic plates lay on top of a wooden box, on one of the lower shelves. Curiosity got the better of Viola once more. She removed the plates and opened the box. Inside was a collection of more glass plates. Each was too large for the standard camera in the studio but a perfect match for the larger format of the camera before her.

She picked up one of the photographic plates, stepped back into the sunlit studio and held it up to view the image more clearly. It was a delightful scene of children playing hopscotch.

This must be one of the Magic Lantern plates.

Without warning the children moved. Viola gasped. She fumbled to catch the glass as it almost slipped from her fingers.

Surely her imagination was playing tricks on her?

Viola inspected the image more closely, keeping a tight grip on its wooden frame. She had not been mistaken. The children were indeed moving. One child slowly turned his head towards her, opening her mouth in a silent cry.

Viola gasped. *It moved! What if the other images also move?*

She darted back into the store room and ferreted through the box. She found the desired image and returned to the studio. A sickening chill crept over her body. She bit her lip as she reluctantly held the plate upwards allowing sunlight to illuminate the image.

There, in all their glory, sat Lord and Lady Hearst. Viola's grip tightened as she steeled herself for the impossible. Her heart raced as the couple startled and jumped up, seeming to stare directly at her in a plea for help.

Viola froze. Her eyes widened. She swallowed, trying to wet her dry throat.

How could this be? Surely it is my imagination?

The front door closed, the thump shuddering the silence. The voices drifted in from the hallway. A second door closed. The wooden floor boards quivered under her feet, each approaching footstep fluttering through the soles of her boots. The voices grew louder.

Viola stuffed the glass plate into a large pocket inside her cashmere visite and concealed herself behind the copious velvet window curtains. She grabbed the tail of her overskirt and wrapped it across her body, making sure to tuck her bustle in close. She held her breath and waited.

Viola watched as Brewer directed Doctor Collins to the sitter's chair. George followed them into the room and locked the door. He glanced at the doctor and frowned.

"I recommend using the new camera, Mr Brewer," said George. He approached the chair and started to clamp the doctor's head in the metal contraption. "You must sit perfectly still, sir." He positioned himself behind the chair to finish securing the restraints. "It takes several minutes to complete the exposure. You don't want a blurred picture."

Mr Brewer shot a glance in George's direction. Unseen by Doctor Collins, George silently mouthed that their sitter worked with the police. Brewer remained calm and wheeled the camera away to make room.

"I think you are correct George. It will suit our purposes better," he said.

Viola remained motionless behind the curtain. She heard the camera being rolled away and watched them set up the replacement.

She considered her situation. Doctor Collins was effectively immobilised. She was a lone woman, hampered by her bustle and restrictive corset, against two, possibly armed, men. Her muscles tensed. Her fingers trembled.

No you don't. Not my Henry.

She clutched at her skirts. As if in answer, her hand knocked against the tiny pistol she had discovered earlier.

It's loaded.

At least she was now armed.

Viola extricated the gun from its hiding place and took a deep breath. Brewer rammed the glass plate into position inside the camera. Viola strode out from her concealment, drew back the pistol's hammer and aimed. George turned in response to the noise. He froze.

"Move away from the camera, sir," said Viola, gesturing with the gun.

Neither man moved.

Doctor Collins tried to stand. His body refused to move. He twisted, trying to loosen the head-clamp's grip. His feet floundered, tangling in the drop cloth beneath the chair. With Doctor Collins of no offensive value, Viola had no option. She squeezed the trigger.

Both men jumped to avoid the shot. They need not have bothered. It missed its mark.

"Viola!" yelled Doctor Collins. He struggled to free himself from his entrapment.

Viola cursed the loss of her eye and the resulting lack of depth perception.

One bullet left. She was going to make her second shot count.

George was the first to his feet.

Viola aimed again, compensating for her previous error. She squeezed the trigger a second time. George grabbed his leg and fell to the floor, in pain.

"Good shot," said Doctor Collins, as he continued to loosen the metal clamp.

"I was aiming for the head!"

Brewer rose to his feet. He smiled. No more bullets. No more haste.

Viola was not about to let a photographer win. She did something no one, including herself, had expected; she launched herself towards the camera. In a flurry of blue silk and skirts, she slid along the floor.

Viola's pleated train caught up in the tripod leg, overbalancing the top heavy apparatus and sending the camera toppling to the floor, and silencing Brewer's laugh short. She slid to a halt at Doctor Collins' feet.

There was a crack, a flash. Then silence. Thick acrid smoke enveloped the room. It rose slowly and drifted up through the open sky light. The smell of sulphur lingered.

Viola coughed, gasping for clean air. She glanced around the room.

Doctor Collins spluttered. They were alone.

Doctor Collins cursed as he finally freed himself from the grip of the head clamp.

"Explain to me what just happened," he demanded as he helped Viola to her feet.

Viola motioned to him to fetch the camera. He did so, keeping it at arm's length, and placed it on the desk.

"You are not going to believe me." She sighed with relief and handed him the notebook. She then slipped the glass plate from its sheath and held it gingerly.

Doctor Collins flipped through the notebook and sighed.

"Optics is *your* speciality."

THE END

Doctor Jack

Chapter 1: Marylebone

eavy rain battered against the window of the carriage. Water rolled down the pane. There was nothing but darkness beyond. The carriage shuddered to a halt. A flash of silver tapped against the glass.

The Man in Grey folded up the evening edition of The Star and tucked it under his grey felt bowler, which sat on the seat beside him. His grey-gloved hand eased the carriage door open a crack. The tassels edging the roof twitched in the breeze, barely visible under the gas lighting of a nearby street lamp. Faint notes of Westminster Quarter filled the cab, as tiny droplets of water whipped the padded leather seat opposite.

"Well...?" he asked.

The silver head of the cane appeared in the opening, as the bells started their countdown. A small, red droplet rolled off the tip and fell to the floor.

One...

"It is done," whispered the cane's owner, through the crack. He remained camouflaged by the ongoing downpour outside.

Two...

"Good," said the Man in Grey. "That should provide an adequate distraction. It will be best if you removed yourself from Whitechapel."

Three...

A disembodied grunt replied from the dark.

The Man in Grey slid a note through the crack. The paper disappeared into the inky void.

Four...

"Take this to our office in Marylebone, and do try to keep out of trouble," said the Man in Grey. "A month should suffice."

"I have work to keep me busy," came the reply.

Five...

"Don't get too enthusiastic," said The Man in Grey. "Your real work will begin on your return."

The door clicked shut, as the bell tolled six. The Man in Grey shook some errant droplets off his boot. Small red stains slowly seeped into the cab's carpeted floor. He retrieved his copy of the evening newspaper and continued reading as the carriage rattled along the cobbled streets of the East End.

Doctor Viola Stewart sat in her Drawing Room. The morning sun danced across the rosewood table as the breeze tugged playfully at the lace curtains. She tugged at her brunette curls as she read her book, which had been sent to her by her dear friend Doctor Doyle.

There was a soft knock on the Drawing Room door.

"Miss?" said Polly as she nudged opened the door. "Doctor Collins has arrived. Shall I bring tea?"

"Yes, Polly," replied Viola. "I'll wager he will fancy some of your cake as well."

Polly bobbed slightly and returned to the kitchen.

The tall, and rather dapper, figure of Doctor Collins filled the doorway. He swept off his bowler and executed a stylish bow in one smooth movement.

"Good morning, Viola," he beamed.

"Good morning, Doctor Collins," Viola replied.

"What are you reading my dear?" he asked.

"A detective novel," she replied. "Doctor Doyle sent it to me."

"Ah, how is Arthur doing?" he asked.

"He is considering a trip to Europe."

Collins leaned over Viola's shoulder, allowing his hand to rest gently on her arm. "More detectives. I have my hands full now. I wish he would not encourage you in such reading matter," he sighed.

Viola smiled. "If I remember, all three of you were almost inseparable in Edinburgh. Donell was always complaining he never had time to study."

"That was your fault, Viola. You were a distraction. I am surprised he took so long to ask you to marry him," he replied, his eyebrow arched. "Mind you, if he had dallied any longer, I would have asked you myself."

Viola felt a warm flush over her cheeks. Collins sat down next to her and smiled.

Polly cleared her throat, waited a few seconds, and entered the room.

"Tea and..."

"Your lovely cake," continued Collins. "What have you got for me today, Polly?"

"Fruitcake, sir," she replied.

"Excellent!" He clapped his hands together and rubbed them in delight.

"If that will be all, miss?" Polly replied.

"Yes, thank you Polly."

Polly curtsied and left the two doctors to their own amusements.

"So to what do I owe the pleasure of your company today?" Viola asked.

"Ah, I thought you may want to accompany me to a private exhibit. My colleague Sir Archibald Huntington-Smythe has returned from Paris and has brought back a wonderful prize," he replied. He leaned back into his chair and took a long sip of his Darjeeling tea.

"What prize?"

The doctor's moustache twitched as he smiled briefly, took another quick sip of tea then replaced his cup on the low table.

"A Benz Patent-Motorwagen Number Three," he replied.

"The one that drove one hundred and twenty-one miles?" Viola bit her lip as she caught the gaze of her guest. "You are teasing me, aren't you?" she asked.

"I am serious." His piercing blue eyes glinted. "He has agreed to let us accompany him on a drive."

"Oh!" Her china cup rattled faintly on its saucer. Viola placed it gently on the table next to the doctor's cup.

"When can we go?"

"We are invited to afternoon tea."

Viola took a deep breath and sighed.

"What do I wear for a ride on a horseless carriage?"

Viola stepped onto the footpath. Her companion, Doctor Collins, paid the cabby and sent him on his way.

Sir Archibald Huntington-Smythe lived on Harley Street, not far from Collins' practice, in a four story red brick townhouse at the end of the row of upper class dwellings. White stone edged the windows lining the facade, and matching stone wedges graced the doorway. A decorative scalloped iron fence and large glass-paned windows attested to the success of the doctor.

Collins smiled, opened the iron gate and escorted Viola to the front door. A shiny brass plate announced Sir Archibald was a specialist in biometric mechanical technology.

"Looks like he does exceptionally well," said Viola. "But I wonder, how can injured workers afford his services, or the permits required for mechanicals or modifications?"

"He has only the best clientele," replied Collins. "Of course, the title also encourages them. By Royal Appointment, as it were."

"I would have thought there would be a limited demand for his expertise in technological limb replacement amongst the elite. There are not many limbs lost in the course of luncheons and balls, surely?" asked Viola.

"Now, now. Sir Archibald is a good fellow. He does what he can. It is not his fault the law restricts use of mechanicals. The Queen has her reasons," he said. "I am sure it is for the good of the Empire." He knocked on the door.

A smartly dressed butler greeted them.

"He is expecting you, Doctor Collins."

The interior of the house did not disappoint. The entry hall was spacious. Custom-made tessellated tiles decorated the floor. Damask silk wall covering and exquisitely carved furnishings lined the walls. An engraved brass plaque directed any prospective client towards his professional rooms to the right.

Viola unwound the scarf from her large brimmed hat, and passed it to the butler. He ushered Viola and Collins up the carpeted stairs and into an equally opulent private parlour lined with portraits. Several display cases boasted a grand array of equipment and academic curios covering many scientific disciplines.

So this is not just to impress patients.

"Good afternoon, Doctor Collins," said Sir Archibald.

"Good afternoon," replied Collins. "May I introduce Doctor Viola Stewart of Greater Marylebone Street? She is an excellent oculist."

"Pleasure to meet you, Sir Archibald," said Viola. "May I thank you for the opportunity to view the Patent-Motorwagen? I hear you brought it all the way from Paris."

"Yes, yes." Sir Archibald clapped his hands and adjusted his spectacles with his long, slender fingers. "An oculist, you say? Wonderful. Please sit." He lowered his tall frame onto one of the velvet-padded chairs. "Tell me, do you make your own lenses?"

Viola nodded.

"Excellent, Doctor Stewart. Have your read about the new tracking telescope?"

Viola smiled and nodded. *Not only was he an aficionado of cutting-edge biometric mechanical technology but he had an ardent interest in optics as well.*

"Yes, in California, Sir Archibald."

"You will appreciate the effort required in perfecting the optics." Sir Archibald chuckled.

"Thirty-six inches in diameter. It is astounding. I hear the Royal Society is petitioning the Queen for permits," said Viola.

"Wonderful," Sir Archibald rubbed his hands together. "You see, our friend Collins prefers the biological sciences."

Viola laughed. "But he does excel in his field."

"That he does. He has helped me with a few conundrums."

Doctor Collins nodded and smoothed down his moustaches. "Only too pleased to help, Sir Archibald."

All this talk of optics. Poor Doctor Collins.

"Good chap." Sir Archibald grinned. "Now, Doctor Stewart, would you like to see one?"

"A conundrum?" asked Viola.

"A tracking telescope, my dear Doctor," replied Sir Archibald.

Violas eyes widened. *It would never fit here.*

"Where...?" she asked.

Sir Archibald grinned and pointed toward the roof. "It is a scaled down model but I can assure you it is a perfect working replica."

Viola nodded enthusiastically. She loved new scientific gadgets almost as much as she loved detective stories.

"Thank you, Sir Archibald. That would be most intriguing," replied Viola.

"You are very welcome, my dear," replied Sir Archibald, "and after the telescope viewing, could I tempt you with some afternoon tea, before adjourning to view my vehicular acquisition?"

Viola fidgeted with the brim of her hat. *A Motorwagen, a tracking telescope. What other treasures do you own? I could never afford such things, or secure the permits. The advantages of being allowed to practice medicine, no doubt - and a man. Viola bit her lip. One day I'll be allowed to practice medicine and not have wasted five years study. At least I was awarded a science doctorate. If only optics paid better. I'd be able to afford to get a permit to own my own Motorwagen.* If only London society could accept her as an equal.

"Will there be chocolate cake?" asked Collins.

"Ah yes, I do remember your fondness for all things cocoa," said Sir Archibald.

Afternoon tea brought with it a symphony of smells. It was a grand affair with meticulously cut sandwiches, elaborate pastries and richly decorated cakes. A faint smell of rose wafted up Viola's nostrils as she lifted her teacup to her lips. Sir Archibald glanced at Viola as she sipped her tea. Viola smiled back politely.

"I hear you have been conducting research at the London Hospital," Collins remarked. Sir Archibald's attention wavered, his gaze flicked back to Collins as the conversation was redirected to his favourite subject.

"Ah yes. Did you know that there has been a revolution in photographic plate technology? A gentleman named George Eastman has engineered the most ingenious flexible transparent film, which can be wound into a portable camera!" he replied.

Viola pursed her lips and raised her teacup to her lips. She took a long sip, hoping to conceal her disdain. She had nothing but bad experiences with photographers

"How is photography related to your work in limb mechanics?" asked Collins. He shot a quick glance in Viola's direction.

Viola knew he was aware of her aversion to photographers.

"Glad you asked, Collins," Sir Archibald replied. "Doctor Stewart may be interested as well." Sir Archibald turned his attention back to Viola.

"How so?" she asked.

"Do forgive me, Doctor Stewart but..." Sir Archibald tapped his right eyelid and smiled weakly. "I do not mean to be impolite. As a woman of the ophthalmic sciences, you may be interested in some of the latest research."

Viola's eye widened. Her hand flinched, as she resisted the urge to touch her eyepatch. She sipped her tea in earnest.

Collins cleared his throat and carefully placed his cup of tea on the low table before them.

"With such advances, there is speculation as to the possibility of human ocular transplantation. I have been recently approached by a benefactor willing to fund research into the area," Sir Archibald said. "With the technology striving ahead, I have no doubt we will find the solution."

Viola managed a feeble smile. Sir Archibald was an eminent doctor in his field. She could understand his enthusiasm. If she had not been so afflicted, perhaps she would not have been embarrassed. Collins had described him as a friend and seemed to hold him in high regard. There must be more to this man.

And he seems quite happy to share his new gadgets with me.

She straightened the rose-coloured eye patch that covered her injury.

She would remain calm.

Collins' brow fleetingly crinkled as he watched Viola. He took a sharp breath.

I wish he wouldn't be so protective.

"Shouldn't we adjourn to the Motorwagen before our light fades?" Collins suggested.

In the centre of the small courtyard, behind the townhouse, stood the Patent-Motorwagen Number Three. The carriage was dominated by three wooden-spoked wheels, which made it resemble an over-sized and over-appointed three-wheeled velocipede.

A tall handled rod was attached to the unsprung front wheel, to provide steering. The leather-upholstered bench seating sat on top of a large wooden box in which, Viola surmised, the engine was housed. A leather canopy was neatly folded flat behind the seat.

Viola quite forgot her previous discomfort as she drank in the smell of the new leather and was transfixed by the shiny cylinders and brightly coloured flywheel at the rear of the horseless carriage that stood before her. If only she could ride in it!

"How fast does it go?" she asked as her gloved finger traced along the wheel's rim.

"Ten miles an hour," replied Sir Archibald.

Viola's finger froze on the wheel. "Ten!" she gasped.

"Impressive," replied Collins. He drew a deep breath, and straightened his lapels.

"Shall we proceed?" asked Sir Archibald.

"Yes please," said Viola, as she draped her shawl over her wide-brimmed bonnet and wrapped the remaining material around her neck. *I have never felt more ready to proceed, in my life.*

Sir Archibald slipped on his leather gloves then opened the box nestled under the carriage's seat. He grabbed at the large metal flywheel and yanked it towards him. The engine chugged once, and there was silence. Sir Archibald leaned his body into the flywheel and spun it again.

This time the wheel continued to spin. The engine jiggled inside its wooden casing. A clicking noise accompanied each revolution as the pistons quickly fell into a rhythm.

Viola sat between the two gentlemen, watching Sir Archibald's ritual as he prepared for them to move. His left hand hovered over the long brake lever. His right hand rested on the half wheel that crowned the steering rod that lay directly above the front wheel.

Viola slipped on her goggles, which would serve to both protect her remaining eye and hold her wrap in place over her bonnet. It was preferable to remain orderly at all times, especially when motoring in public.

Her heart raced as the contrivance jolted forward, rolled into the laneway and rumbled over the cobblestones of Harley Street.

Viola's eye widened. She concentrated on the breeze that caught her fine silk shawl, as its edges gently caressed her face. She could hear the rhythmic chugging of the engine beneath her; no jarring clatter of horse hooves to spoil her reverie.

The bench seat rattled as the Motorwagen entered Cavendish Square. The Wagen lurched as the wheels hit a particularly uneven part of cobblestones. The seat momentarily dropped beneath Viola. As gravity returned she plopped back onto her seat, bumping into Collins, and jolted back into her present situation.

The mechanical carriage continued south along the west edge of Cavendish Square. Several ladies huddled under their parasols and

whispered, pointing excitedly at the motoring party. A gentleman, in a long coat and top hat, looked up from his evening paper and adjusted his spectacles. He sighed and watched them pass.

"Would you like to take the wheel, Doctor Stewart?" asked Sir Archibald, as they turned left along the south edge of the square. Viola gasped, too surprised to reply.

"That may not be advisable," said Collins.

Viola's smile fell. Her joy crumpled into disappointment. *Is he questioning my ability to handle a mechanical device?* She bit her lip and turned to her friend, searching his face desperately for any clue, any explanation for his publicly voiced scepticism in her abilities.

His blue eyes met her gaze, then widened. A small furrow creased his forehead. He held her gaze, as his mouth opened, and he shook his head.

You know me better than that.

"What I meant was your unfortunate lack of depth perception, given your monocular state," he hastily added.

Her smile slowly returned.

"Never less, I am determined," she said, as she grabbed at the steering wheel, hitting it with her fingertips. *Damn my eye.* She straightened her back, reassessed the distance and took charge of the steering wheel. She grinned and turned the wheel anticlockwise as they reached the west end of the square.

"Oi, bloody Toffs! That bloody contraption oughtn't be allowed on the streets." yelled a dark-suited man as he stepped off the footpath. He jumped back, almost colliding with a second man in a long dark coat. The second man pulled his billy-cock hat low on his face and strode off, as the carriage continued northward.

Collins grabbed the edge of his seat.

"Some people cannot handle progress," said Sir Archibald, as they turned left along the south edge of Cavendish Square.

"Maybe they just don't understand it," replied Viola. She winced, as she narrowly missed a startled flower seller who had craned her neck in search of the missing equine power.

"Research cannot stop in an effort to pacify the uneducated masses," replied Sir Archibald.

"Watch out!" yelled Collins.

Viola dodged an oncoming horse-drawn carriage. The horses snorted in protest and reared. The driver's face contorted, his scream left behind them as the Motorwagen sped onward.

"Thank you, my dear," Sir Archibald placed a steady hand on the wheel. "I think it may be time for you to return to the Police Station morgue, Collins," he continued. "You don't want to neglect that body for too long."

"What body?" asked Viola, her enthusiasm for the conversation renewed.

"Ah... yes," replied Collins. His mouth wrinkled.

"Another murder. The second one this week," replied Sir Archibald.

"Two?" Viola glared at her friend. "When were you going to tell me, Doctor Collins?"

"I did not want you jumping to conclusions with all of the shenanigans in the papers."

"The papers?" Viola turned to face Collins. "You mean the Whitechapel Murderer? Has he been here, in Marylebone?" she whispered.

"No, he hasn't, and we don't want the newspapers thinking he has," replied Collins. "We have enough unease in London, as it is."

"I could deliver Doctor Collins to the Station. I am attending a Research lecture this evening. Perhaps you would accompany me to the lecture, Doctor Stewart?"

"I appreciate the invitation but I will be assisting Doctor Collins at the morgue." Viola flashed a smile at Collins. "Thank you, Sir Archibald."

"As you wish, my dear. I venture you are braver than most women."

Sir Archibald turned the Motorwagen eastwards, towards Wigmore Street.

Viola examined the victim's eyes. Even in the coldness of the Marylebone Station morgue, the woman's cornea was already starting to grow cloudy.

"What time did she die?" she asked Collins.

He checked the report papers. "Around midday," he replied

"We could have tried making an optogram, to view the murderer," Viola sighed. She placed her hand over the body's face and closed her sightless eyes. "There is no chance of getting any result now."

"For someone with such an intense dislike for photography, you have a strange obsession with optograms, my dear." Collins chuckled, then hummed quietly, as he scribbled more notations in his case book.

"Was the Motorwagen a distraction to keep me from finding out about the murders?" Viola wiped her hands on her apron.

Collins avoided her glare. He closed the torn flesh over the exposed organs of the victim, covered her body with the linen sheet, then busied himself with returning the room to order.

Viola tapped her foot on the tiled floor of the morgue.

"You cannot deny that the injuries are consistent with those in The Whitechapel Murderer victims," she continued. "The neck wounds, the mutilations?"

"There are also inconsistencies," Collins replied calmly. "It is unlikely he would venture this far from Whitechapel, besides Whitechapel Station agrees that we have seen the last of him. It has been weeks since the last murder."

"Perhaps we have an emulator?" said Viola. "We should let the Whitechapel Constabulary know about them."

"No."

"But..." argued Viola.

"No, Viola." Collins raised an eyebrow and eyed her. "They have enough problems, trying to quell the riots. They do not need rumours of another murder to fuel even more. We don't want unrest spreading throughout London and here to Marylebone."

Viola removed her apron. She looked into his pale blue eyes. They seemed to have lost some of their usual brilliance. *He is worried.*

"Just promise me one thing," she said. "If there are any more murders let me know immediately, so I can make an optogram, and please reconsider telling the Whitechapel Constabulary?"

"That is two promises, Viola." Collins nodded. "I promise." His eyes confirmed he was telling the truth.

"Beautiful day for a picnic," said Collins.

Viola smiled at him as their carriage sped along Harley Street.

"Perfect," she replied. "Can we go any faster?"

She would always want adventure. How could he compete with that? He redirected his attention from the well-stocked picnic basket, back to his companion.

Viola fingered her eyepatch; it matched her purple gown immaculately. Dark curls framed her face, falling over her eyepatch, hiding the scars and accentuating her pale skin.

She was as beautiful as she was intelligent, exceedingly so. Collins had admired her wit and charm since their first meeting at Edinburgh University. She had been one of the few women allowed to study medicine. She outclassed most of the other students. It was despicable to him that London society would not allow her to practice in her profession.

Unfortunately for him, Viola had noticed his friend Donell Stewart first. And Donell had noticed her. A lot. He had been Donell's Best Man and had remained their friend after University, even moving to Harley Street to share a practice with Donell - and to remain close to Viola. He had been there to support her when Donell died, and when she took over his secondary practice as an Oculist in Greater Marylebone Street. He valued her friendship more than any man's.

It had been a long wait for him. Two long years. Too long. At least she was no longer condemned to wear the colours of mourning. She was too young to be a widow. But perhaps she had spent too much of her time in his company? He was starting to hear the whispers.

The picnic basket thumped against his leg, as the carriage jostled over an uneven patch of cobblestones. Wine sloshed in the bottle tied to the basket. The smell of freshly cooked chicken and aged cheese wafted throughout the carriage.

The doctor grasped the edge of the carriage seat. And if they did not slow down, people would do more than just whisper.

"I do wish we could slow down."

Viola laughed. He loved watching Viola laugh. The corners of her eye wrinkled slightly, her mouth turned up most attractively and her chest bounced ever so slightly.

Viola took a deep breath and leaned toward the open window, drinking in the biting wind. The carriage slowed. The wind settled into a flutter. Long tendrils of hair played across her face, licking at her neck.

Not quite as exhilarating as the Benz-Motorwagen though.

"I would love to have a Motorwagen of my own," said Viola. It had been a thrill to control the mechanical carriage. No horses to lead them. She could go where she wished. *Free.*

Collins leaned towards Viola and cradled her hands in his.

"Viola, the Benz-Motorwagen costs one thousand pounds," he said.

Her eyes widened. "Oh dear. Maybe I will have to settle for one of those new motorbike contraptions," she replied.

"Only if you promise not to fall off," he said.

Viola tugged her *visite* tighter, blocking the early autumn chill creeping along Harley Street. The sun dipped low, rimming the roof line and lengthening the shadows of the buildings. It had been a grand day out. The picnic had been perfect, the company convivial and the food exquisite.

Collins accompanied her on the leisurely stroll back to his townhouse. Viola gripped his arm; the picnic basket graced the other. His feet clicked briskly as he strutted along the footpath beside her, his head held high. His broad smile wrapped around her, warming her against the chill.

A rotund lady in a black bustle dress and bonnet nodded as she passed the couple. "Good afternoon, Doctor Collins. Good afternoon, Doctor Stewart," she said. Her brown eyes twinkled as she smiled at them. "It is good to see you both again."

"Good afternoon, Mrs Caulder," replied Collins.

Did she wink at me? Viola blushed.

Mrs Caulder swished her bustle as she continued on her way, and disappeared into one of the townhouses off Cavendish Square.

A stout gentleman with sandy hair emerged from the nearby alley, to their right. He wore a long dark coat and billy-cock hat. His walking cane swung in his hand as he hurried across the street. He pulled down his hat as he reached the footpath.

There is something familiar... Her heart lurched.

Viola watched as the figure strode along the square towards them. *I*

knew someone once... A pain seared through her gut. *Please, not...*

"... Findlay?" Viola whispered out loud.

"Pardon?" said Collins.

"Is that Findlay?" she replied.

The man was now only a few feet away

"I don't think so," said Collins. His eyes narrowed as he scrutinised the man's broad face hidden under the sandy moustache. "It could be." His eyes widened. He lifted his hand to his mouth: "Findlay!"

Viola tugged gently at his jacket, and shook her head slightly; "No, I was mistaken. Let's go."

The man lifted his head towards them, searched the surrounding streets before tipping his hat. He smiled; a crooked smile that made Viola feel ill.

"Henry Collins, why am I not surprised to find you on Harley Street?" Findlay nodded his head in Viola's direction. "Miss Viola Carrington," he said. He glanced at their entwined arms. His smile dropped fleetingly, only to return with a renewed passion. "Or should I say Mrs Collins?"

"Ah..." replied Viola. She shook her head and extracted her arm. "Mrs Stewart, actually."

"And where is dear Donell?" Findlay asked.

Viola did not reply.

"Donell Stewart was buried over two years ago, Findlay," whispered Collins, as they shook hands.

Findlay tilted his head to one side, turned to Viola and narrowed his eyes.

"Such a pity, for one so young." he said. His gaze skimmed over the eyepatch.

"How wonderful to meet you again, Mrs *Stewart*." Findlay bowed, with unnecessary flourish, his gaze never parting from her face. His hat jiggled as he straightened and nodded briskly.

Viola swallowed. She avoided his stare, letting her gaze fall to the ground.

A faint jangle issued from under his sleeve. Viola glanced at Findlay's gloved hand. *Was that a glint of bronze near the cuff?* Findlay smiled and clasped his hands behind his back.

"Mr Findlay," acknowledged Viola, with only a glimpse. She took a half-step backwards, placing Collins between them.

"Doctor Findlay now," he replied. "But I preferred it when you called me James, Viola."

Still the same ill-mannered cad, lacking in basic social etiquette.

"You returned to study then? Not at Edinburgh?" asked Collins, as he straightened his shoulders.

"No," said Findlay, "Europe. They are much more open minded on the Continent."

"Where do you practice, Findlay?" asked Collins.

"Whitechapel. I work at the Royal Hospital and do a bit of work with the poor and homeless. Someone has to see to them," he replied.

"What finds you here in Marylebone?" asked Collins.

There was a pause.

"Research," Findlay finally replied.

"Did you attend the Research lecture last night? A friend of mine mentioned something about a venture into Surrogate Ocular Enhancement," said Collins.

Findlay's attention lingered on Viola, eyeing her up and down slowly.

"Yes, that is it..."

Viola's head spun. A rushing sound echoed through her head, muffling Findlay's voice, and Collins' reply. Slowly the noise faded, until she heard nothing but a buzzing echo. The hairs stood up on her arms. It was as if thousands of insects were crawling under her skin, racing each other to escape his unwelcome scrutiny. She eased closer to Doctor Collins, out of Findlay's line of sight.

Viola had befriended James Findlay, in her first year at Edinburgh University. He seemed so fragile, so lost. *If only I had not felt sorry for you.* Now there was no pity left.

She had been initially flattered by his interest, unrequited though it was. Flattery soon turned to discomfort when his obsession became obvious. *Thank goodness Donell had been there.* Findlay's attention had eventually wandered elsewhere. If only she had known earlier to whom he had transferred his affections.

It was all my fault.

Now Findlay had returned, as had the unwanted attentions. There was no Donell to protect her now; Collins had no idea of what had passed.

I hate you.

"... yes, fascinating." said Collins. Something nudged her elbow. "Perhaps Doctor Stewart would like to accompany us?" His voice calmed the crawling insects.

"An excellent idea, Collins," replied Findlay.

Viola returned her attention to the two men and ventured a quick glare in Findlay's direction.

Findlay clenched his hands. There was a faint click. Viola remembered those hands. She shuddered. *I hate you, for what you did to my sister.*

"You are uncharacteristically quiet, Doctor Stewart," said Findlay. One corner of his mouth curled up. "You used to be the life of the party, if I remember correctly. Did married life tame you?"

Viola sucked in a quick breath and returned to Collins' side.

Where is my sister?

"Doctor Collins also works with the Marylebone Police," Viola said, hoping to catch Findlay off guard, and provide a veneer of security for herself. *I will not respond to your taunt, you...*

Findlay shoved his hands in his pockets and looked Viola directly in the eye.

Where is she?

His cold blue eyes seemed to accuse her of betrayal.

Viola swallowed. *Why should I feel guilty? You are the guilty one.*

He blinked slowly and turned his gaze to Collins. "You always were good at dissections, Collins."

"As were you, I recall," replied Collins.

"Anything interesting of late?" asked Findlay.

"Two murders in Marylebone," Collins replied. He screwed up his nose. "Not pretty."

"Like yours in Whitechapel," said Viola.

Findlay shot a quick glance back in her direction.

Did he flinch?

"Doctor Stewart seems to think they are similar to The Whitechapel Murderer's handiwork. She has an idea on how to obtain the identification of our local killer."

"How so?" asked Findlay, his attention now directed at Collins.

Viola let out a slow, quiet breath, now his vile grey eyes were occupied elsewhere. A reprieve for her lungs. Her hands gripped Collins' arm tightly.

"She intends on making an optogram, if we are unlucky enough to have another murder. We may be able to catch an image of the villain, possibly get an identification," explained Collins.

"You have an interest in eyes, Doctor Stewart?" asked Findlay.

"She is an excellent Oculist," replied Collins.

"I suppose that is not surprising given..." started Findlay.

"Given what?" snapped Viola. *Given I'm not permitted to be doctor?*

Findlay's gaze flickered back to Viola, skimmed over her left eye then settled on her eyepatch.

"I could fix that for you," he declared.

"Fix what?" asked Viola. *You will not lay a hand on me.*

"How did you lose your eye, Viola?" he asked. The crooked smile had returned to his lined face.

Viola's chest tightened, a thread of ice shot up her arm and stabbed the empty socket concealed under the eyepatch.

She slowly stepped back, this time finding scant comfort in the shadow of her friend Collins. Her right hand went up to her lace-edged eye patch. Her fingers trembled slightly as she adjusted the accessory that seemed so offensive to him.

"Now see here, Findlay. You may be an old friend but that is not a question a gentleman should ask." Collins stepped forward to meet him. He stood a few inches taller than Findlay. Collins looked down to him and hissed. "I will not have you embarrassing Viola."

Findlay clicked his tongue. "I excel at research, Collins," he replied, his teeth gritted behind unmoving lips. His jaw muscle tightened.

Collins pulled Findlay to one side and turned his back to Viola.

A gallant effort, but not effective. Viola listened unobtrusively.

"We both know that transplant technology is not *that* advanced. And when you give up or fail? What then? "

"Why fear failure, Henry? How can you fail, if you do not even try?" Findlay replied.

"I will not condone you giving her false hope. I think you should be on your way, *Doctor* Findlay."

Collins' grip tightened on Viola's arm. He placed his hand on Viola's, its warmth flowed up her arm.

Viola bit her tongue. She did not need anyone to fight her battles for her but... She looked up at Collins.

Thank you, Henry.

Findlay spun on his heel. The tip of his cane tapped on the footpath as he strode off to their left. Something jiggled on his billy-cock hat. Something Viola had not seen as he had stood near her blind side. Icy tentacles gripped Viola's heart. She froze. A small feather jutted from the hat band, its shaft half wrapped in silver thread. *A red feather.*

James slid into a nearby alleyway and watched Viola and Collins march along Harley Street. He watched as they entered Doctor Collins' townhouse. He remained there a few minutes more, a half smile frozen on his face.

James turned and made his way along the alleyway into the growing darkness of early evening.

I always did like those green eyes.

A loud knocking echoed through the dim hallway. Polly straightened her skirts before she opened the front door - her white cap in one hand, the fire poker in the other. She could still see the street lamp flickering through the slit between the front curtains.

"Who is it? Tell me or I shall call a Constable," she declared.

"Doctor Collins," came the muffled voice. "I am sorry for the early hour."

Polly relinquished the poker, and opened the door. Collins' tall dark silhouette was outlined in a golden glow, as the sun rose above the roof tops. He removed his hat and greeted Polly cordially. His smile quickly faded.

"There has been another murder."

Viola greeted Collins as she dashed down the hall stairs. Her hand ran along the balustrade to steady herself as she eyed him through a heavy eyelid.

"You did say you wanted me to tell you *immediately* there was another murder," he said.

Viola nodded and buttoned up her coat.

"They found the body less than fifteen minutes ago and are taking it directly to the morgue. There may have been enough light for the optogram."

"We must hurry," replied Viola.

"Your equipment is already in the carriage."

"Ask Miss Blake to cancel my morning appointments, please, Polly," Viola said as Collins whisked her towards the waiting carriage.

The morgue was shrouded in a red light, casting a bloody appearance onto the linens that covered the body lying on the autopsy table. Viola clicked her fingers in the direction of Constable Jones.

"Careful you don't let any unfiltered light in, Constable Jones. It will bleach the retina before we can even begin," she said.

Jones nodded. He remained silent, hardly glancing up as he followed her strict instructions for the setup of the equipment. Several shallow dishes were arranged along the side bench beside the wall. He placed a large glass bottle of Alum alongside the other bottled liquids, at the end of the bench.

Viola glanced at Jones, as he propped up a camera-like box on its wooden tripod, at the other end of the room. He placed a selection of glass plates on the table.

Viola busied herself preparing the dissection area, trying to ignore the ache in her right eye socket. A photographic record would preserve the retina from the rough handling it would be given by the Police. *There is no other option.*

"Thank you, Constable Jones. Please ensure no one enters until we are finished," instructed Viola.

"Yes, ma'am," replied Jones. The door clicked shut behind him.

"Let us hope there was enough light when she died, to activate the

Visual Purple," said Viola. She licked her lips, and took a deep breath. *We only get two chances to make this work.* The edge of the scalpel glistened as she took it in hand, and nodded for Collins to remove the sheet that covered the victim's face.

He flipped the linen to reveal the woman's face. The eyes were gone. Two cavernous orbits stared back at her. Viola's heart sank. *No chances.*

"How...?" she gasped

"A coroner's knife, by the look of the cuts," replied Collins.

"No, I mean how did he know?" replied Viola.

"I would say he is a surgeon."

"Obviously." Viola's knife clattered onto the workbench. "But why take the eyes now? It is as if he knew what we were planning." Viola leaned against the bench. *Not fair!*

"There is no way the murderer could know what we were planning," He gently placed his arm around her shoulders. "It is a coincidence, Viola."

Viola shook her head. "Don't try to dissuade me. I will find the answer. I am a scientist, after all." Viola did not believe in coincidences.

"I will tell Constable Jones to put the equipment away, so we can do the autopsy," he said. "We may find something on the body itself."

Viola appreciated every opportunity Collins gave her to practice her medical skills. They had become a little rusty with disuse. *It is fortunate that she is already dead.* She grabbed a clean scalpel and pierced the pale skin. Viola smiled. Collins glanced at her, rolled his eyes and returned to his work.

She found the work both satisfying and strangely relaxing, helped along by the soft, melodious humming of her friend. She often found herself ruminating on her detective novels or retracing memories in the peaceful surroundings. Many ideas surfaced during the sessions. She smiled as she remembered the kerfuffle caused by her jaunt in the Motorwagen. She had only narrowly missed the man in the billy-cock hat. *The hat band had sported a red feather.*

"Findlay!" she exclaimed.

The doctor's normally steady hand jolted forward, just missing his own wrist. He dropped his knife and staggered back in relief, falling onto a chair behind him.

"Viola!" he scolded.

"It is him. He knew."

"Knew what? What is this obsession with him, Viola? You weren't yourself when we met him yesterday." He shook his head. "Was there something between you and him?"

"Nothing," replied Viola. She continued to examine the body. Hoping that would be an end to the conversation.

"I thought now you were free to..." Collins rubbed his moustache and stared at the scalpel on the floor. "No, don't tell me. I don't think I want to know. Perhaps I was mistaken about us."

Us? Viola shook her head and resisted the urge to throw her hands up in the air.

Collins straightened his collar, took a deep breath and swallowed.

"What happened in Edinburgh?" he asked.

"We don't talk of it," she said.

"Who doesn't talk of what, Viola?" asked Collins.

"My family doesn't talk of my sister Anne," replied Viola.

"Your sister? Didn't she elope with some Scottish Lord?"

Viola's scalpel clicked softly as she placed it on the marble-topped bench. She placed both hands on the edge of the table, avoiding his gaze. Her heart raced.

"I wish she *had* eloped," Viola said. Collins nodded.

Viola stared at the lifeless body beside her. Blood pooled at the foot end of the table and dripped into a large, metal bowl on the floor. *Red blood.*

"That summer she came to visit, do you remember?" Her lungs

tightened under an unseen weight. Viola's hand slipped from the table. Her fingers were stiff, her hands clammy. She rubbed her hands together trying to warm them.

Collins wrapped his arm around her shoulder. His fingers pressed gently on her arm, warm and reassuring. Her heartbeat slowed and the weight on her chest lightened.

Viola looked up at him. His blue eyes held her gaze and would not allow her to look away. Small, familiar, comforting creases formed at the outer edges. He caught her bloodied hands and held them tight. A faint smile flickered across his lips.

"We will get you a cup of tea," he said calmly. "Then you can tell me what happened."

They sat in one corner of the morgue, the doctor gently wiping Viola's hand free of autopsy remnants. Slowly, methodically. It had a calming effect on Viola, allowing her to recount the tale.

"After her visit, Anne talked about an admirer. She always kept him a secret. She loved the adventure. Two months later she told father she was returning to Edinburgh to visit me. She never arrived. I should have never introduced Anne to Findlay."

"Surely, you can't blame him? He was our friend," said Collins.

"We found love letters, written to Anne. I am sure they were in his hand," replied Viola.

"Was there any proof he was responsible?"

"Nothing but the letters. But he left University the following day. I know it was him!" she said.

"Donnell never mentioned anything."

"Father told him after we got married. Donell promised not tell anyone," replied Viola.

"That explains why he avoided Findlay, after second year." Collins let out a quick breath, and rubbed his forehead, leaving behind a smear of blood. "You never spoke of him again either. I just assumed it was because you were too busy after he left University." He stood and wiped his bloody hands on his leather apron. "Still, you can't accuse the man of murder just because you suspect him in your sister's disappearance. You need proof," he said.

Viola's teacup rattled as she set it on the table. She rose from the chair and crossed her arms.

"No, this has nothing to do with Anne. Listen. He lives in Whitechapel; he is here at the same time as our two murders. The wounds from both sets of murders are consistent. The very day after you inform him that we intend on obtaining an optogram, there is a murder where the eyes have been removed, by a doctor. It is him." She paced the room, clenching and unclenching her hands.

"Coincidences. The killer could be anyone with knowledge of the knife, a butcher for example." Collins frowned and shook his head. "I can't believe it is Findlay. He always seemed a decent chap."

Viola froze. She looked Collins directly in the eye.

"He cannot be trusted," she pleaded. *How did he get my red feather? What if Anne had not been in Edinburgh? What if it had been me?*

Viola renewed her hold on his hands, and squeezed.

"What if...?" she gasped.

"Don't think about it, Viola." He pulled her towards him and embraced her. His touch was warm and reassuring. Viola felt her muscles relaxing. She took a deep breath. She could smell him - a sweet smell with a hint of formaldehyde.

"We need to contact Whitechapel Station," she whispered.

"I agree," he replied.

Viola watched Doctor Clark remove his apron and throw it into the hamper, next to where Doctor Collins stood. Clark shook his head.

The Whitechapel Police Surgeon had sent his assistant to ascertain if there was any link between the Marylebone murders and those of the Whitechapel Murderer.

He couldn't bother coming himself.

Clark washed his hands in the bowl provided, and slowly wiped them dry.

"Your report is very thorough, Doctor Collins. I understand your..." He raised his eyebrow and shot a glance in Viola's direction, "assistant was adamant you contact us?"

"Doctor Stewart is a colleague, a local Oculist. She is a specialist in optics," replied Collins.

"That may be..." Clark began.

"If you can confirm this as one of his, then the Whitechapel Murderer will be responsible for four murders," said Viola.

"They are calling him The Ripper now. Have you not seen the papers? The fools have published a letter. All hell is breaking loose," grumbled Clark as he scrutinised her.

Viola stared back, not flinching from his gaze. She did not condone the ignorance of the established patriarchal medical establishment. Her necropsy skills were as good as, and possibly exceeded, many of the registered doctors. She had attained second in her dissection class at Edinburgh, studied Taylor's *Manual of Medical Jurisprudence* and assisted Collins for the past two years. Her only disadvantage had been the randomness of conception. *I will not apologise for genetics.*

The doctor's eyes flicked to the cold body on the table, then back to Viola. He smiled.

"You are correct. The slices to the throat area are identical - left to right. Some of the mutilations are present." He turned and lifted the linen sheet to reveal the victim's torso. "The eyes are new. They are not consistent with either of our murders."

"We believe a Doctor James Findlay of Whitechapel is responsible,"

Viola said. She swallowed. Would he believe them?

"Reasons?" Clark asked.

"He was present in both areas, at the time of the murders. He does medical research at the Royal Hospital, so has the expertise suggested by the injuries, and has recently taken a keen interest in research in eye transplants," said Collins. He stroked his moustache, avoiding Viola's gaze.

"And he knew I was going to make an optogram of the next victim." Viola added.

"Optogram?" said Clark. He scribbled in his notebook. "Worth a try. Have you expertise in the area?"

"I have been studying the area for a few years now. I could set up the equipment at Whitechapel easily enough, if you requested." Viola replied.

"A doctor, you say?" asked Clark.

"Passed the final medical exams in Edinburgh," Collins replied.

"Not allowed to register," Viola whispered.

"Then finished a Doctorate in optics," continued Collins.

There was a silent pause as Clark slowly closed his notebook.

"Then you could be of help, Doctor Stewart," he said. "I will send word if we need you. However, I am hoping that will not be necessary. The Inspector thinks we have seen the last of the Whitechapel murders."

"So you do not think our two murders are related?" Viola asked. Her brow wrinkled.

"Perhaps. It could be someone copying the Ripper? All the details were published in the evening papers." Clark tsked, shook his head and frowned.

"Will you not investigate Findlay?" Viola asked.

"We will interview him, but I cannot promise anything. Let's hope this is an end to it. We are having a hard time trying to control the unrest. If it continues, we will have more rioting on our hands. I wouldn't let any reporters get wind of your theories, Doctor Stewart. You would not want the same unrest here." Clark retrieved his bowler and nodded to them both. "Good evening, Doctor Collins. Pleasure meeting you, Doctor Stewart."

Chapter 2: Whitechapel

A trickle of light filtered through the soot-coated windows of the Whitechapel Police Station. Doctor James Findlay sat in the far corner of the reception area. He hated waiting.

He ran his hands along the rim of his billy-cock hat. His finger caught the edge of the red feather that was tucked in the band. The hard edge of his scowl softened, one corner of his mouth curling up slightly. He caressed the tufted edge of the feather. Its softness rekindled memories of a simpler time.

Sweet Viola. His finger froze. His scowl returned. *And the life I never had.*

James placed the hat on the chair beside him. The front door swung open, momentarily illuminating the reception room. The fetor of stale beer wafted in his direction.

James surveyed the room's inhabitants. Drunkards languished on benches awaiting relocation into cells until they were deemed sober. Two over-dressed prostitutes argued with the Constables, as they were dragged through the doorway and ushered to the Desk Sergeant. The reek of cheap perfume trailed behind them. A man in a grey suit and bowler chatted to the Desk Constable who scribbled in the large notebook that lay before him.

A corpulent, balding, middle-aged man entered from one of the doors to the back rooms. He sported a thick moustache and bushy mutton chops. A gruff-looking Constable accompanied him.

"Oh, Inspector Abberline," cooed the older prostitute. "Have you returned to us, dearie?"

The middle-aged man glanced in her direction, not deviating from his undertaking. A glimmer of a smile flickered over his lips. He whispered to the Constable and disappeared back into the maze of rooms beyond the door.

"Doctor James Findlay," announced the Constable.

James donned his hat, tapping it gently into place. A few of the less inebriated drunkards raised their heads, with interest.

"The papers said he was a surgeon," one slurred.

"'Ere, they got 'im," replied one of the harlots.

"Nah, not him," said another. "Couldn't be. He's a doctor at the workhouse."

James followed the Constable. He smiled as he slipped through the miscreants, side-stepping the roving hand of a prostitute.

James sat opposite Inspector Abberline, a large oak desk between them.

"Good evening, Doctor Findlay," said Abberline. He stubbed out his cigar and carefully laid it in the top drawer, then motioned to the Constable to close the door. James could hear feet shuffling behind him.

"I still don't know why I am here," said James.

"I don't believe that for one minute, Doctor," replied Abberline.

James took a long slow breath. He was not going to be caught up in the growing frenzy that permeated the East End these days.

"We are interviewing all the local doctors. Maybe you have seen something, heard something?" Abberline continued.

"The papers say you suspect The Ripper is someone with medical training," said James. "I cannot believe someone in my profession could have such disregard for life." James steepled his fingers and placed them to his lips.

"Never the less, I need to know where you were on the nights of the thirty-first of August, eighth, twenty-fifth and twenty-eighth of September. If you would be so kind?" replied Abberline.

There was a slight pause as James considered the dates.

"Twenty-fifth and twenty-eighth?" He lifted his eyebrow and looked directly into his interrogator's eyes. "The papers have not mentioned any more murders."

"I never said there had been," replied Abberline. "Just answer the question, Doctor Findlay."

"Very well. I was attending a lecture on transplant research, in Marylebone." A faint smile crossed his lips. "I met a few friends when I was there."

"Ah, yes. Can you give me their names?" asked the Inspector.

"Doctor Henry Collins and Mrs Viola Stewart, both of Marylebone," James said.

"And the twenty-eighth?"

"On the twenty-eighth I was meeting a prospective benefactor. Research is expensive and I don't make the gilt like my colleagues in Harley Street. We dined until extremely late and he offered me hospitality for the night. Given the hour, I took advantage of his generosity. Very nice digs, they were," James chuckled. "And I am afraid I had too much wine."

Abberline plucked up his pen and tapped the nib on the side of the well.

"Name?" he asked, his pen poised above his notebook.

"Mr Grey of Marylebone." James leaned back in his chair and watched Abberline jot down more notes.

Abberline leaned forward.

"And the nature of your research?" he asked.

"Medical transplants," replied James. He dropped his hands, fingers still interlocked, to the desk and leaned forward. "The possibilities are without limit, Inspector. If I could successfully replace a diseased organ - a liver, an eye - then many deaths could be avoided."

Abberline grimaced. "A bit fanciful, don't you think?"

"No. There is a limb specialist in Harley Street who uses mechanicals for his work. Replacing internal workings with mechanicals would be fanciful. Why try to recreate something already perfected? The key is the blood. I am sure of it."

"Where do you perform this research, Doctor Findlay?" Abberline asked.

"The Royal London Hospital," James replied. "Ask for Doctor Oppenshaw."

More scribbling ensued in the notebook until a sharp knock on the door echoed through the room. The attending Constable slipped into the corridor. He returned a few seconds later brandishing a note for the Inspector. Abberline grumbled and snapped his notebook shut. He read the note, frowned, and tucked it into his notebook.

"Thank you for helping us with our enquiries, Doctor Findlay. Constable Barlow will see you out," he said.

"Glad to be of help," said James.

He tipped his hat and followed the Constable through the corridors to the reception room. The man in grey nodded, almost imperceptibly, then left. James smiled and followed.

A slurred voice drifted through the door as he left: "I told you it weren't him."

It was always late afternoon when James visited his benefactor's residence, a large house with a decorative brass knocker, which bordered

a well-kept park.

Orange light spilt over the red patterned carpet and busy yellow wallpaper which graced the parlour. Several exquisitely carved dark-walnut chairs gathered around a polished parquetry table. The deep upholstered velvet glowed a brilliant red. Shelves, dripping with curios and Oriental Objets d'art, surrounded the fireplace.

James sank into a chair and stirred his tea, careful not to let the spoon touch the sides. He smiled at the man, in the perfectly tailored grey waistcoat and suit, sitting opposite him.

"I would have preferred Darjeeling, Mr Browne," James said.

The man chuckled. "I suspect you prefer gin," he said.

"Alcohol dulls the brain," replied James. "I cannot do my work with slowed reflexes."

"Hmm," replied Mr Browne, avoiding James' lingering stare.

James smiled. People found it disturbing when he looked them directly in the eye. It seemed to unnerve them, compelling them to avoid him. He could become invisible by asserting his presence. *One did not wish to be noticed when in the employ of the Men in Grey.*

"Our man has informed me that Mr Grey has been interviewed by the Whitechapel Constabulary. They are satisfied with the alibi he provided."

"I never doubted the efficiency of The Society," James replied.

"As they do not doubt yours," his colleague replied. "I have your further orders. There will be two more." He sipped his tea. "The newspapers have been very obliging with stirring up the lower classes. Of particular note was the recently published letter. Perfect."

"Your work, Mr Browne?" asked James.

"No." Mr Browne shook his head. "But we do intend to capitalise on the growing unrest. Do you know Dutfield's Yard?"

"On Berner Street?"

"Yes. Mr Smith will meet you there, when you are finished. Say about one o'clock? Make sure to get a trophy. I have some business to attend to before sunrise. We intend to stir the pot a little more." Mr Browne chuckled.

"Any requests?" James stared into his tea. The sunlight reflected off the liquid and caught in his eyes. The aroma enveloped his nose, flooding his sinuses. It reminded him of more pleasant times in Edinburgh.

"Any local tart will do," replied Mr Browne. "Just make sure it appears connected. Multiple killings stir up the underlying anxiety that brings out the terror in the masses. The more dissent we can rally, the better for the cause." Mr Browne's eyes flickered in James' direction. "We need to undermine the population's fascination with their Fat Empress. We want them baying for her blood when she cannot provide them with the safety they think they deserve."

James lowered his cup. His eyes glinted.

A deep gong echoed along the hallway, as the clock struck six.

Mr Browne's attention snapped back to his beverage. He wriggled in his chair and adjusted his shoulders.

James reached for a piece of cake.

"And the final task?" he asked.

"We have been having problems with Miss Kelly. She has been trying to blackmail The Society." Mr Browne snorted. "The doxy has threatened to tell the authorities about our arrangement. She has refused to supply any more information without significant extra payment. I am afraid Doctor John Williams, and The Queen's secrets, are now lost to us."

"Pity. It was convenient having access to someone inside Court. And Doctor Williams?" asked James.

"As far as I know, he is unaware of her betrayal. He will not expose himself nor his indiscretions. Once we tie up the loose ends, further action will not be required." Mr Browne sighed. "Best leave a week between them. We want to prolong the agony of the miserable rabble."

"Maximum fear with minimum carnage?" said James. He smiled.

"You will be, as always, supplied with an alibi."

"There is one problem," said James. His smile faded for but a second. He was confident that Viola and Collins had been behind his visit to Whitechapel Station.

Damn her eye!

"Deal with it, Findlay. You are good at that," Mr Browne said. He finally returned James' gaze. "Oh, and when it is complete, you owe me a new pair of boots," he said. "It is difficult to get blood out of leather."

James had supper, collected his tools and wandered along Commercial Road in search of a playmate. It had been raining steadily for much of the evening. Beads of water dripped from the brim of his hat as he dodged ever-growing puddles, past the street-sellers huddled under the eaves of makeshift booths. He evaded the sharp umbrella tips of those unfortunate enough to find themselves caught in the weather.

James continued on his way. Any one of them would be too much of a risk, either in view of potential witnesses or with efficient defence weapons at their fingertips.

Though inconvenient, the curtain of rain would help provide cover. He pulled up his collar, and tugged his hat low to protect him from both the continuing downpour and errant gazes. No one would be suspicious of a man in a long coat and wide-brimmed hat. He preferred working in dismal weather.

James made his way south in search of quarry. Unsuccessful. The rain also had its downside. Many of the punters had sought shelter; the streets were empty. He turned along Ellen Street. There was usually more Tail closer to the railway yard.

A muffled scream echoed faintly around him.

Someone was having fun.

James ignored it. It was not an uncommon occurrence in London. Above the sound of the rain, James could hear quickening footsteps along Berner Street. He ducked into the shadows, pulling his hat low to hide his face.

A tall man dashed past him, then disappeared down Ellen Street in the direction of the railway lines. James waited. More footsteps echoed along the street. A second man darted down Ellen Street.

James reached for his pocket watch.

A quarter to one. Time was running out.

He stuffed the watch back in his pocket, and strode north in the direction from which the two men had come. The rain pelted softly on his hat. He scanned the darkened street and listened for footsteps, alert for the opportunity he needed.

He heard another faint cry as he reached Fairclough Street. Opportunity had knocked, and it had provided both suspects and a witness.

"Leave her alone!" yelled James.

The man jumped back from the gateway, shot an angry look in James' direction and ran off.

Perfect timing.

The woman flattened against the gate. Her eyes narrowed.

"Doc?" she whispered.

"Long Liz?" James smiled and moved closer to his quarry. He could feel his pocket watch against his chest.

Tick. Tick.

Time was running out. The patrol could be along soon.

"Are you hurt?" he asked.

"No, dearie," Liz replied. She straightened her chequered neck scarf.

James put an arm around her. He could feel the layer of moisture that clung to her brown velveteen bodice, peeking from under the long fur-trimmed coat.

"It has been a long time since I have seen you at the clinic," he said calmly. "Let me check you were not hurt."

Long Liz sniffed and wiped a rain drop from the end of her nose. She nodded.

James ushered her through the gateway. The surrounding buildings thwarted the light of the half moon, trapping Dutfield Yard in pitch blackness. The click of Long Liz's heels echoed off the walls. The sound of rain trickling off the roof edge greeted them. Not a soul responded to their trespass.

Tick. Tick.

In the darkness, James' friendly smile dropped. A determined grin crept over his lips. He wrapped his fingers around the knot in Liz's scarf. He pulled tight, constricting her windpipe.

Long Liz clawed at the scarf, digging her nails into his gloved hand. A sharp pain shot through his shin where her heel connected.

He dragged her further into the yard. He flicked his hand. A long blade snapped out from under his sleeve, the ring of steel cutting through the rain. Another flip of his wrist. The handle was in his hand. The blade was at her throat.

A hint of light peered over a roof top as the moon rose higher. The knife's edge barely shimmered before clouds buried the moonlight again.

Tick. Tick.

Another swift movement, below the jaw. She stopped fighting. The tension fell from her body. A dead weight pulled on the makeshift garrote. James released the grip on her neck scarf. She slumped to the ground, at his feet.

Tock.

There was a clattering just inside the side door.

James pushed the body against the cellar's barred window. A faint light flickered from within. He darted across the yard, slipping behind the cover of the large wooden gate. And waited.

The weak glow from the cellar lamp licked the edges of Liz's fur-trimmed coat, drowning in the darkness beyond the body. It danced momentarily and withdrew back into the building.

He listened. *Nothing.*

The drips from the roof edge slowed. He shook his head. A flurry of drops fell off his face.

A lone gong chimed one o'clock from within the bowels of the nearby Men's Club. *Out of time.* He was late for his appointment.

Another bank of cloud settled in, large enough to stifle the moon's attempt at revealing his incomplete work. James pushed the gate forward slightly. Just enough time to collect a trophy for his employer.

There was a clatter of shod hooves on the cobblestones, a rattle of harness. In the dark, he could hear the snuffles of a horse, less than a few feet away. He could smell its stale breath.

Too close.

His finger pushed a button on his wrist. The blade slipped back under his sleeve.

The horse froze in the gateway. The harness rattle became frantic. It fussed, trying to back out of the yard.

The crack of the whip almost deafened James.

"Steady, boy," the driver grumbled.

Silence.

"Who is that? Get up," the driver demanded.

No answer.

The cart jostled. The driver's hob-nailed boots scraped on the stones as he moved towards the body.

"I've no time for gin soaks."

More scraping, then footsteps running towards the Men's Club.

The yard would soon be full of men. He stood no chance against a crowd, clamouring for blood. His blood. He could not wait any longer.

He stepped back into the yard. He slipped past the cart, through the gateway and turned right.

James could hear the cries in the yard, as he hastened along Berner Street. He turned into a laneway, striding ever further away.

Heavy, measured steps echoed around him, as he reached Batty Street.

Were they up ahead? James glanced back. Or behind?

The dark cloud resumed its march across London's sky. Faint moonlight trickled through the chinks. A tall figure walked directly towards him. Its pace quickened as it moved closer. James flicked his wrist. His blade descended, its bloody tip resting on his fingertips, concealed behind his hand.

"Good evening, sir." The low voice emanated from below a Constabulary helmet.

James took a calming breath and smiled.

The constable's eyes flicked down to James' coat. Blood.

"Doctor Findlay?" he asked.

James tensed; the edge of his blade pressed into his palm. He searched the street. They were alone.

"Mr Browne sent me. Constable Smith at your service, sir."

"You are late," James sighed.

"There were a couple of men hanging around outside the yard. I had to continue my rounds," Smith replied.

James pressed the button on his wrist contraption. The blade slid silently back into place. The tip of his finger was wet. He flicked the remnant of blood away.

"A Police Constable?" asked James. *The Men in Grey have spies everywhere.*

"Yes, sir."

"Whitechapel?"

"Yes, sir." Smith looked past James, towards the growing sounds of the commotion. "We had better move, sir. I need to return to my beat. I am due back here in about ten minutes."

They made their way along Batty Street.

"Mr Browne will meet you at Aldgate East Station, directly. He has some urgent business for you," said Smith. He pressed a bundle of clothing into James' hands.

James nodded. Perhaps there would be another opportunity for obtaining the requested trophy?

"Good evening, sir," said Smith.

James watched Smith trudge along his beat on the way to Berner Street, then turned and headed toward Whitechapel Railway Station where he could change clothes.

James followed the empty tracks from Whitechapel Station, and emerged from the tunnel into Aldgate East Station. He scanned the platform. He was alone. He hopped over the tracks and bounced up to the platform. His wide-brimmed hat slipped off onto the ground. A size too big. James picked it up, dusted it off on his trousers and climbed onto Aldgate platform. *The Men in Grey aren't perfect, after all.*

Mr Browne stepped out of the shadows to greet him.

"No cane tonight, Findlay?"

"Not when I am working," replied James.

Mr Browne held out his hand.

"I believe you have something for me?" said Mr Browne.

"I was interrupted," James admitted.

Mr Browne's moustache twitched. He shook his head.

James shot a cursory glance over the station and lowered his voice, "But our friend, *Mr* Smith, said you have some urgent business for me to attend to. So it looks like I have another chance to procure an item for you.”

“You are in a good mood,” said Mr Browne.

“I love my work,” James replied.

“Maybe not tonight,” replied Mr Browne.

“I can’t see why not. I like urgent business.”

“Your friend Kate Eddowes has been into the gin again. She has been asking about a reward for the Whitechapel Murderer,” said Mr Browne.

Jack sighed.

Oh, Kate. He had known her through two husbands. He had helped deliver one of her children. She comforted him on those rare occasions he was struck by remorse.

“One of your drinking buddies?” asked Mr Browne

“A ... patient,” replied James.

“With some generous benefits, I gather.” Mr Browne chuckled.

James frowned. He was not accustomed to being on the other end of the Men in Grey’s information gathering network. How much did they know? And what would happen when he outlived his usefulness?

“Bishopsgate just let her go. We can’t have her talking. There is too much at risk, Findlay. I want you to sort it out. Tonight.” Mr Browne slapped his bowler back onto his head.

She’s often around Prostitutes Island after a bender.

“She’ll be near St Botolph’s,” replied James. “She will need more money.” He bit his lip. *Tonight it is.*

“Meet me back here when you are done.” Mr Browne adjusted his grey bowler and returned to the shadows. “And I will need that trophy.”

The night was clear and crisp, after the rain. James thrust his hands into his pockets to warm them against the autumn chill. A gentle breeze tugged at his loose coat. Not his usual style.

James skipped over some puddles left by the earlier downpour. It would have been a pleasant midnight stroll to St Botolph's, if he was not on such serious business.

The church's white stone quoins glowed dully under the clearing sky. James noted the windows that encircled the tower. The provided an excellent view of the streets that surrounded it on three sides.

St Botolph's had stood, almost unchanged, for over two hundred years. It had witnessed many secrets for centuries before that. James did not intend for it to witness any more tonight.

Kate is a friend. We need privacy.

A woman, dressed in dark red rags, tottered towards him.

"I can show you a good time," she slurred.

The smell of rotten fruit engulfed him. James grimaced, pulled his cap low over his face, and raised his hand in declination.

"Your loss," she chuckled. She continued on her promenade around the *Island.*

As she turned the corner, another woman strolled into view. James could hear her singing. It was a sweet and jolly tune.

He caught his breath. His heart fluttered unwillingly. It was Kate.

How many times have you sung me to sleep? How many times have I run my hands through your dark auburn locks? How many times have I asked you not to return to the lodging houses?

The flounces on her skirt bounced playfully as she walked closer.

I will miss her.

"Kate," he whispered, as she drew closer to him.

"James?" She smiled.

"How was hop picking this season?" he asked.

"Bloody awful. I need some cheering up."

"Planning to earn some gilt another way?"

"Maybe?" she replied in a lilting voice. She clicked her tongue.

James reached around her waist and pulled her in close. She was not wearing her stays. He smiled.

"Feels like you are ready for some fun?" he said.

"Always for you, James," she laughed.

His gaze flicked up to survey the church windows. Too many. *Not here.*

"I know a place," he said. He pulled his cap back over his eyes.

They walked, arm in arm, along Duke Street then entered Mitre Square via Church Passage, passing under the lantern at the edge of the square. Kate's quiet singing echoed through the empty space.

She reached up and played with the brim of James' hat. Her chin wrinkled as she pouted.

"No pretty red feather? Did you lose it?" she asked.

James shook his head. He flicked a glance over the surrounding buildings. Workmen would not be at the warehouse at this hour. He led her across the square, away from the lanterns and into the shadows. James smiled. *Viola would not be happy.*

Kate giggled as he snuggled his cheek into the soft fur that trimmed her collar.

"I know," he whispered.

"Know what, James?" She serenaded him with another tune.

"What you said at Shoe Lane," he replied.

"What, dearie?" she said, between verses.

"Did you say anything at Bishopsgate?" James asked. His voice was calm and measured. His smile was gone.

"The gin robs my memory."

"What have you been saying about me?" he hissed. His grip around her waist was unrelenting.

"I said nothing." She was no longer singing.

"You are an intelligent woman, Kate. That is what I love about you." He squeezed tighter. "But you always have such bad taste in men."

"I didn't give them my name," she whispered.

"Whose name did you give them, Catherine?"

"Mary... Mary Kelly," she whimpered.

"You should not have done that, Catherine."

"I don't know who she is. I swear." There was fear in her eyes.

His blade rested in his hand, half out of its sheath. James hesitated. Her hair smelt of honey. His heart raced.

"The gin does not rob your memories. It wakes them up. Problem is, it loosens your tongue as well." He held her close and gently kissed her neck. "You know the rules. Whatever you hear, you never tell. I am so sorry, my sweet. You should have said nothing."

Kate's eyes widened. She stared directly at him. Her lips parted in a silent reply.

A pain shot through James' chest as slivers of ice stabbed his heart. A fleeting wave of nausea rushed over his body. He took a sharp breath. Then it was gone. His heart beat slowed until he could not distinguish it from the beats of his pocket watch.

He could see the glint in his eyes reflected in his blade. There was blood already on it. His eyes faded. His pupils dilated, leaving only a sliver of blue visible. James closed his eyes and let his arm fall across her neck.

Kate's body tensed. She didn't scream.

His scream was silent, constrained. He stood up, checking the square for intruders. There was no one.

He glanced down at the body lying at his feet. In the darkness, he could see still see the cheery flowers on her skirt, now covered in red stains.

She was going to tell. I had no choice.

James squatted beside the body to finish his work.

There would be no more singing tonight.

James arranged the entrails neatly, tore off a piece of her apron, then stood to inspect his handiwork.

It is done.

He could not bring himself to look into her eyes, or what was left of them. It had been necessary; he knew Viola would insist on interfering. He could not allow her any satisfaction.

Blood formed rivulets and washed away along the cobblestones underfoot.

So much blood.

A tear rimmed his eye.

He turned and fled.

James peeled off the blood soaked coat. He rolled it up tightly and carried it under his arm. There was too much blood on it; he could not risk wearing it in the streets, even at this early hour. The cut-away coat he had worn under it was less conspicuous. He pulled at the jacket, with its hidden treasure-trove of gadgets. He straightened the sleeves and buttoned it up tight, then slipped out of the Square.

James sobbed quietly as he made his way to Aldgate Station. His gaze remained forward. He would not look back. Their song had ended. His work must always come first.

He paused outside the underground station. The clouds had finally cleared allowing wisps of fog to creep up to the doorway. James scanned the street. It was empty. Those who enjoyed the late hours would be more interested in other endeavours. Even the street sellers had given up on the night trade, leaving no one to witness his ingress.

Mr Browne was awaiting him on the platform. He checked his pocket watch, as James approached him.

"You look tired," said Mr Browne.

James did not reply. He handed Mr Browne the corner of Kate's apron, a string still attached and spotted with blood.

"This will serve the purpose," said Mr Browne.

James remained silent, staring at the linen remnant. He could not tear his eyes away from it. He remembered the Michaelmas daisies and golden lilies on her green chintz skirt that she had worn under the apron. They matched her hazel eyes. Those eyes that stared back.

It had to be done. For the good of the many.

His chest tightened. The muscles in his arms and legs tensed.

You ordered it, Browne. James' blade slid silently from its sheath, well-lubricated from use.

"You should be careful who you befriend, Findlay," Mr Browne continued, unaware of the blade nestled in the palm of James' hand, awaiting a decision.

"Yes," James said coolly. He struggled to slow his heart beat. The tension flowed from his arm into the blade.

Shrieking laughter drifted down onto the platform from the street above, followed by scuffing footsteps and voices. The moment was gone. There was calm. The blade retracted back into James' sleeve.

The apron was whisked out of sight. Mr Browne tipped his bowler, made his farewell and slipped off into the shadows, a large wedge of chalk in his hand.

James jumped down and jogged along the tracks. Once he reached the tunnels, he hurled his cap into the darkness.

Viola paced the parlour.

"Why haven't they sent word?" she said.

Collins shrugged. He poured himself a second cup of tea. His fingers fidgeted as he reached over a bundle of letters to liberate a piece of Polly's finest fruitcake from the silver tea tray on the table beside him. He avoided any attempt to initiate frivolous conversation when Viola took to her restless room ambulations.

Viola halted and thrust her hands onto her hips.

"If you keep eating all of Polly's cake, you won't be able to fit into those lovely tailored waistcoats you are so proud of," she said.

He straightened his vest. It hugged his torso in all the right places.

He has an excellent tailor.

Collins popped a piece of cake in his mouth and turned his attention to the pile of letters, neatly tied with a fine red ribbon. Three more letters lay scattered beside the neatly stacked cache, partially covering the morning newspaper which announced another Ripper murder. The letters were partially unfolded, having been thrust into Collins' view then hastily dropped by Viola before she continued her rounds of the parlour.

A knock on the front door echoed through the hushed room. Viola rushed to the window that overlooked Marylebone Street. She knelt on the window seat, pressing her face against the glass as she tried, unsuccessfully, to get a better view of the front door.

Polly tapped on the Drawing room door, sending Viola into a further flurry. She spun away from the window, plopped herself down on the window seat then straightened her silk skirts. She took a deep, calming breath.

"Yes, Polly?"

Polly entered. She bobbed her head in their direction, and presented a letter to her mistress.

"Thank you, Polly," said Viola.

Collins nodded in return, raised his cake-filled hand towards her and, with a sly smile in Viola's direction, scoffed the cake. Polly bit her lip, unsuccessfully trying to stifle her giggle, and scurried back to work.

Viola ripped the letter open, as she returned to her chair by the tea table. She scanned the note. Her eyelid widened briefly, flickered and then squinted. Her mouth opened, closed, then opened once more. She read the note a second time before breaking her silence with a faint screech. The letter fell to the table and nestled amongst the other discarded missives.

"What is the matter?" asked Collins.

"They've dismissed him as a suspect," Viola grumbled. She abandoned her seat to resume her pacing.

"Who? Findlay?" Collins retrieved the letter from the table and studied it carefully.

"Why will they not believe me?" she said.

"Viola, Inspector Abberline says here that he has an alibi. There are witnesses. There's no way he could be in two places at the same time."

"The witness lied," replied Viola.

"Why do you doubt him?" Collins asked. "He is a bit odd, I grant you, but he has always been a respectable man."

"You don't know everything," Viola whispered.

"Viola..." His voice was calm. "Tell me about Findlay."

"It is personal," she replied.

"More personal than the family secret about your sister?" he asked.

Viola turned. She opened her mouth, paused, then closed it again. She twisted the ring on her finger.

"I met him when I was in first year," she replied. "He had no friends. I decided to rectify that. I wish I hadn't." She paused, took a breath then continued. "He kept following me. I asked him not to. Honestly, I didn't encourage him," Viola pleaded.

"It only stopped after the summer Anne visited." Viola took a sharp breath. "I should have realised something was wrong."

Collins' tea cup, precariously poised mid-air, finally tipped from lack of attention. He cursed under his breath, as the hot tea poured over his leg. His widened eyelids soon crumpled in anger. He turned towards Viola

"I didn't know," he said. His brilliantly coiffed moustache drooped low on both sides. "Donell and I assumed he was a friend of the family."

Viola began fidgeting with her hands. Tears streamed down her face as she prowled the room.

I am sorry, Anne.

Collins slowly rose from his chair, his gaze locked on Viola as she circled.

"Viola...?"

She did not reply.

He crossed the room to Viola. He took her hands in his and waited.

Viola avoided looking her friend directly in the eye. She did not need her friend's sympathy; she needed his support. She wanted a chance to prove herself in the Whitechapel investigation - a chance to chase down her daemon and prevent him from hurting any more women. Most importantly, she needed a chance to find out what happened to Anne. Only Findlay knows the truth.

I need to know what happened.

Viola's hands twitched.

Collins released Viola's hands. He straightened his shoulders and snapped his hands behind his back. He cleared his throat.

Viola plucked up the note from Whitechapel Police Station and read it again. She thrust it in Collins' direction.

"Inspector Abberline had an optogram made," she said.

Collins took the note. He glanced at it.

"They say there was no light when Liz Stride was slain, and the eyes of the second woman were cut."

"Why did they not ask me? I could have made it work," Viola said.

"They say the damage was too severe to make a successful optogram," he replied.

"What would they know?" Viola froze mid-step. "They probably got one of their Constables to try it."

Viola snatched the missive from Collins' hand and began reading in a squeaky voice:

"We reserve the opportunity to avail ourselves of your expertise, if there should be any further victim. However, as the Whitechapel Murderer has not been active in the past weeks, we doubt we will need to take this course of action, yours sincerely, etcetera, etcetera."

"Viola, let it be. Let the Inspector do his job," replied Collins. He turned to an occasional table piled high with books. He picked one up and leafed through the pages. "Life is not a detective novel. It is dangerous."

He picked them up, one by one, turning each over and inspecting the spines as he did so. A large notebook sat on the table, by the pile of books. He retrieved it and flipped through the pages. It was full of newspaper clippings of the Whitechapel murders. On the margins of the pages were scribbled notes. Recent news articles quoting the text of the Ripper letters were pasted on the final pages.

"Viola, be careful this does not become a personal vendetta. You could be hurt. As your friend and doctor, I feel it is my duty to protect you."

"You what?" Viola replied. Her fists clenched.

Collins picked up all of the books and tucked them under his arm.

No one takes my books!

"Henry George Collins. Don't you dare touch my books, you malodorous lag. You don't get to tell me what I can and cannot do. You do not own me."

Collins gently replaced the books then held out his hand towards her. "Viola, calm down. Don't be ..."

"If you say hysterical, I will never speak to you again," she scolded.

"I am sorry, Viola. You will always do what you wish but..." He tentatively reached for her hand.

Viola hesitated. "But what?" she said.

"Not all men are equal to your expectations, my dear." He squeezed her hand gently. "If you were to be hurt, I would not forgive myself. I would not know what to do, if I lost you."

Viola's heart skipped as she took his hand.

James dodged the carriages as they clattered along Commercial Street. He had a meeting at the Ten Bells. It wouldn't do to be late. He pulled his billy-cock hat low over his forehead as he passed the Police station.

A young woman leaned against the fluted columns by the Bell's entrance. She was neatly dressed, with a clean white apron. Not the usual tart that frequented the surrounding streets. Her fair hair fell around her shoulders, free from the constraint of any bonnet. She smiled sweetly as James passed her and entered the public house.

The last vestiges of the afternoon sun cast long shafts of golden light across the wooden floor boards. It spilt across the bar, which dominated the centre of the room, and glinted off the patterned tiles that lined the far wall.

The bar-keep circled the room, weaving between the growing number of patrons, as he ignited the gas lamps. A welcoming fire already crackled in the hearth.

The far corner of the room remained in the shadows, concealing the occupant. His grey bowler marked him as James' contact, though his clothes were not up to Mr Browne's usual high standard of attire.

Mr Browne raised his head just enough to catch James' eye. Once acknowledged, he lowered his head returning his attention to his glass of stout.

James collected a pint of pale beer from the bar, and slid through the revelling crowd. He reached the corner just as the lamp was being lit.

"Not here," whispered Mr Browne. "Mr Walden has provided a private room upstairs."

Mr Browne gathered up his drink and coat, and led James up the stairs into a small room, which overlooked Commercial Street.

A tray lay on the table; four pints of beer already awaiting them. James smiled, and sat by the spoils. He hooked his walking cane on the edge of the table and watched the silver dog-headed handle as it rocked slowly.

"Another in your employ?" James asked.

"He is sympathetic to our cause," replied Mr Browne.

"And willing to risk his livelihood, if discovered?" asked James.

"We have many loyal sympathisers, Findlay. Are you reconsidering the risks?" replied Mr Browne.

"Some of us take more risks than others," said James. "All for the cause, of course." He took a sip of his beer.

"Ah, yes, but with much larger compensations. I trust it is worth it?" James smiled.

Mr Browne leaned back into his chair.

"Our little message in Goulton Street has proved more advantageous than we had planned," said Mr Browne. "The Commissioner made the mistake of removing it, in an attempt to placate the rabble. The crowds are now baying for the Metropolitan's blood. They are crying 'conspiracy'."

Both men chuckled.

"My man is engineering to have him removed from office. That should slow them down and let the riots become entrenched," said Mr Browne.

"Then I can resume my work?" asked James.

Mr Browne shook his head.

"Patience, doctor. The Society has decided to let the situation fester. We'll let the papers fan those rumours a little longer."

The smile fell from James' face. "How long?"

"A few more weeks, then you can go play," said Mr Browne.

James winced.

Too long.

His hand trembled slightly as he downed another pint.

Mr Browne watched him through narrow eyelids, then added: "Keeping the Met's resources stretched suits our purpose."

"And if they find themselves closer to my door?" hissed James.

"Their men will be desperately trying to quell the unrest. Besides, they will have their hands full chasing several false clues we have fed them. They have cleared you so there's no need for concern. The Society always protects its own."

James fidgeted with his fingers, circling the thumb around his fingertips. His wrist twitched.

"Can you at least give me more details of my next job. I need to start organising a plan."

"You really do enjoy your work, don't you?" said Mr Browne. "Very well, but promise me that you will not get too excited and disappoint me." Mr Browne paused. "Or The Society."

Mr Browne leaned forward and clicked his tongue. He pointed towards the window.

James crossed to the window and looked out over the street. The nearby buildings blocked out what little there was left of sunset, reducing visibility significantly. The Bell's shingle creaked loudly in the breeze, drowning out the carriages below.

"What am I looking for?" James asked.

"Did you see a pretty young thing on your way in? Very tidy, very agreeable," replied Mr Browne.

"Yes, I thought she was a dollymop."

"She is now. Her Toff has cut her loose. She is now in need of another income," Mr Browne explained. "Just your type."

James shot him a dark glance.

If only I did not need The Society to fund my research.

He took a deep breath, unclenched his hand, then returned to his beer.

"Is the eighth too early?" asked James.

Viola beamed at the two men seated at the table before her. Light streamed into the palm court from the lobby beyond the square columns that surrounded them, partially silhouetting Doctor Collins and Sir Archibald Huntington-Smythe. Nearby potted palms swished in the vestiges of the outside wind, which stole through the door as they opened with each new diner. Viola watched the dancing shadows across the polished tile floor.

Thank goodness The Langham has heating.

An excellent afternoon tea had been set before them, enhanced by the crisp white linen and silver table setting. Viola nibbled on a petite egg and cress sandwich, as she eyed the delicate pastries on the platter on the table before her.

Viola delighted in the afternoon discussion. Sir Archibald had an ingenious plan to take photographic images of astronomical objects, using his new tracking telescope. Viola was relieved once the explanation of the necessary camera equipment was dispensed with. She then listened intently as he regaled them with the intricacies of the mechanics, and to Collins' dismay, the optics of the creation.

Collins picked up a piece of sponge cake and glanced in Viola's direction. He paused. Viola eyed him. His silk waistcoat peeked out from under his jacket. Its silver buttons rose and fell as he breathed.

Very dapper.

Viola's glare softened. A smile flickered over her lips. How could she deny him something he loved so much? She nodded gently. Collins grinned and popped the morsel in his mouth.

He had been quiet for much of the afternoon, smiling and nodding when appropriate. Viola appreciated the effort he had made to ensure she enjoyed herself. He had spent the past few weeks being overly charming, extremely attentive and ever-apologetic for ever doubting her word.

He had taken her to the Natural History Museum and the London Zoo. He had even presented her with a new detective novel. Though he had often admitted that he had no head for optics here they sat, discussing it at length with the Empire's leading expert on mechanics.

Viola smiled as Collins offered her the last pastry. How could she not forgive him? She knew he ached for a change in topic and she had promised not to bring up the subject of the Whitechapel Murders. The poor fellow deserved some relief from the current conversation.

"Tell me about your work in limb mechanics, Sir Archibald," Viola asked.

Sir Archibald's eyes lit up. Collins shifted in his seat and leaned forward.

"At a recent Researcher's Meeting, there was talk of a future technique that may mean that we would be able to attach the prosthetic mechanics directly to the wearer's bone. Of course, there needs to be improvement in the efficacy of current anaesthesia."

"That would be marvellous," said Collins, "but how would one control the attachment?"

"There has been ongoing research, following a Doctor Waller's medical experiments with the innervation of frogs. One of our colleagues, Mr Grey, has been corresponding with Mr Tesla and feels electricity may be the key," explained Sir Archibald.

"Was that one of the lectures at the Meeting in September?" asked Viola.

She shot a sideways glance in Collins' direction. Surely he would fathom the reason for her enquiry but it was unlikely he would create a fuss in public. He may still think her to have an overactive imagination but she knew Findlay was somehow involved in the Whitechapel and Marylebone murders. She had to discover the truth of his alibi.

Collins returned his tea cup to its saucer, with a faint clatter. He met her gaze and narrowed his eyelids briefly.

"As a matter of fact, yes," replied Sir Archibald.

Viola took a deep breath and straightened her emerald silk eye patch.

"Was there any discussion on Surrogate Ocular Enhancement?" she asked. Collins steepled his fingers, resting his index fingers against his lips. He remained silent, his gaze never leaving Viola.

"None, I am afraid, though my colleagues would be very interested in the subject," replied Sir Archibald. "Do you dabble in research, Doctor Stewart?"

"No. Sadly I don't have the funds. However one of my colleagues is considering research in the area." Viola gently placed the remains of her pastry on the plate before her. "You may have met him at the Research Meeting."

Collins ran his fingers over his moustache, then sighed.

I did not promise to stop detecting.

"His name is Doctor Findlay. He studied at Edinburgh."

Sir Archibald frowned and shook his head. "I am not familiar with the name."

"Could he have been a guest at the meeting? About five foot six, broad face, sandy moustache?"

"I doubt it. I am familiar with all the attendees. There was no one there of that description," said Sir Archibald. "Maybe he is known to

Mr Grey?"

Viola popped the last bit of pastry in her mouth. It was sweet and rich. She turned to Collins. He avoided her gaze.

Inspector Abberline would need to be informed of the loss of one of Findlay's alibis. She wondered how many more would prove to be fictitious. Viola smiled.

Collins leaned back into his chair and consumed the last of his cake.

James clutched his leather bag, carefully concealing it under his coat. He walked along Dorset Street and slipped under the narrow arched entry to Millers Court. He paused near a staircase at the end of the narrow lane that led into the main courtyard area. The light from a solitary gas lamp flickered on the door to Mary Kelly's rooms.

Millers Court was long and narrow with several tenement windows facing the communal area. All was quiet.

James remained in the shadows. Occasional drips of water slid off the roof edge and plopped onto his hat.

James preferred the early hours, just past midnight. Passers-by were less frequent. Less interruptions. More time to work. The drizzling rain had continued for most of the night. Even fewer passers-by. He pulled on his gloves, clenched hands and waited.

The rain returned. Small drops tapped on the cobblestones, intermittent at first, increasing in tempo until each tap blurred into a dull hiss.

A latch rattled, just beyond the end of the narrow passageway. From his vantage point, he watched a dumpy, middle-aged woman waddle across the flagstone court, bucket in hand. Faint sploshes of water echoed throughout the courtyard.

James edged further into the shadow of the stairway and pulled his hat down over his eyes, as the woman returned to her lodgings. He waited until he heard the latch bolt click into place before he emerged from hiding and entered the courtyard.

Faint notes of sweet singing drifted through the empty yard, barely audible above the rain. Mary was expecting him. She had been excited when he propositioned her - a Toff client slumming it in Dorset Street.

Probably thought her luck had changed. James' lip curled up at one corner. *She had brought it on herself. No one crosses The Society.* His smile faded. *No one.*

He shoved his bag under his left arm, diligently arranging it so it was still hidden by his coat. He tapped on her door, glanced over the courtyard to ensure there were no witnesses, then entered.

The room was cramped and sparsely furnished with only a bed, two small tables and a dresser. A low fire heated the room. Its flickering glow created golden highlights in Mary's fair hair. Loose curls fell over her exposed shoulder. She had already partly undressed; her clothes were neatly folded on the table near the window.

Mary had considerable personal attractions. She stood as tall as him. She was young, with all the assets which accompanied a beauty yet to succumb to the ravages of the slums. Such were the privileges of having been a mistress to the upper class. James understood how Doctor Williams could be so easily seduced by the lass.

Her blue eyes sparkled as she helped him remove his large overcoat.

"You brought your doctor's bag?' she giggled. A pleasant sound, not unlike her singing.

James let the bag fall on the floor beside the closed door. Mary locked the door behind him and placed the key on the bedside table.

"We won't be disturbed," she cooed.

"We have all the time in the world," James replied.

"I like your hat," said Mary, as she removed it from his head and ran her finger back and forth over the soft red feather which adorned it. "Red is my favourite colour."

"It looks better on my hat, than it did on the bonnet of the original owner," he replied.

"But it is limp from the rain. You can have one of my bonnet feathers if you like," replied Mary.

James took the hat from her, placed it on the bedside table next to the pile of clothes, and pocketed the door key.

He placed his hand on her naked shoulder, avoiding the chemise that skimmed her body, then turned her around to face away from him. Her skin was smooth and unblemished. *Working the streets would soon change that. I will spare her from the curses of her new life.*

He untied the lacing knot for her stays, then curled his fingers under the cord and slowly eased out each loop. He was patient.

"Doctors have such gentle hands," she whispered as she leaned in closer.

"Why is something so pretty as you living in such a forsaken address?" he asked, his crooked smile hidden from her.

James scanned the room. An expensive petite bonnet - such a contrast in the austere surroundings - partially covered a small carved-wooden box that sat on the dresser. Just the right size to store the personal correspondence he had been engaged to retrieve.

Mary twisted her body to face him. Her sharp blue eyes tracked his gaze.

"I like your bonnet," James said, diverting any interest from the box.

"I did not steal it," she whispered. "It was a gift."

"From a gentleman?" he asked.

"John was very generous."

"But not generous enough to liberate you from McCarthy's Court?"

Mary's arms straightened. She pulled her body away, so it no longer rested against his. A small brass key glinted between her breasts.

"He is not like that," she replied. "There are things beyond his control."

"Or do you have other plans?" asked James.

Mary pushed him away and pouted.

"I am sure a pretty lass like you must want for fine clothes and a comfortable house. That requires money or connections. Surely you have a plan to rise above all of ... this?" He theatrically threw his hands wide.

Her gaze flicked towards the box then fell to the floor.

"Yes, but no plans tonight that don't include you." Mary smiled and stared back into his eyes. She let her stays fall to the floor, then softly stepped out of their embrace. She nestled closer to James, then slid her hand under his cutaway coat.

James flinched. He felt the harness of his contraption jolt when her fingers knocked the hidden strapping that secured it.

She gasped, then slowly licked her lips and smiled.

"May I?" she asked.

He saw the gleam in her eye and wondered if Williams had seen it as well. She probably thought she had scored her next rich mark.

James chuckled. *Why not?* He was proud of his work, and she would never be able to use the information. He nodded.

Mary gently squeezed the bicep of his left arm. Her brow wrinkled. She moved her hand lower to his forearm and squeezed a second time. Her eyes widened. A smirk replaced her frown. She reached for his hand and slowly peeled off the glove to reveal a shiny mechanical hand. It glinted fitfully in the light of the crackling fire.

"So, you are slummin' it then?" she asked.

Though mechanical prosthetics were becoming more common, it was only the rich who could, as yet, afford such luxuries.

"Are you really a doctor, or is it for show?" Mary ran her fingers over the metallic digits. "I bet you own a big house."

"I have friends on Harley Street," he whispered.

James did not doubt that her quick mind was already calculating how much money she could extract from him before he realised her true nature. He chuckled at her ignorance. If only she knew his plans for her.

Mary giggled. "I never did a Toff with a mechanical before."

She slid the remaining sleeve off her other shoulder and let the chemise fall beside the stays.

"Take your stockings off," James instructed.

Mary obeyed, sliding them down her thigh, her calf, rolled them slowly off her foot, then presented them to James.

He curled them around his fingers, letting them dangle. With his mechanical arm, he spun Mary around, to face away from him once more. He did not want to look into her eyes. They were the wrong colour.

"Viola," he whispered.

"The name is..."

Her reply was strangled as James whipped the stockings round her neck and pulled taut.

"Murder!" Mary's cry was cut short.

Mary wriggled under his arm. Her struggles grew weaker.

He coiled the stockings around his mechanical hand, slowly tightening his grip. All she could manage now was a faint whimper. Her arms flailed behind her, unable to fight back.

James pulled her closer to him.

"Shush," he hissed.

He nuzzled his nose into her blonde hair. It smelled of roses, reminding him of his younger days and university friendships...

And betrayals.

He flicked his free wrist. The seven inch blade shot out from its exposed sheath. He wrapped his fingers around the handle and closed his eyes.

Mary stopped struggling. The weight of her naked body fell against James. He slipped his arm around her knees and carried her to the bed.

He lay her down gently and twisted his finger through her golden curls. He removed them from her shoulders and placed them over the pillow above her head.

James sighed.

He pulled the brass key from her neck. It chinked against the door key as he slipped it into his pocket.

James placed his hat in his doctor's bag, retrieved his leather apron, and laid out his tools on the bedside table. He ran his fingers along the selection of instruments, and snatched up a scalpel.

He was safe behind lock and key, invisible to the passing world beyond the walls. There was no hurry. He had time to enjoy every minute of his work.

He leaned over the bed. Mary's hair still smelt of roses; a faint metallic aroma mingling with it. He took a long breath, letting the smell fill his nostrils.

He flicked a stray lock of hair from Mary's forehead. He slipped the spoon under one of the orbits. The eye squelched as it separated from the socket. He plopped the blue eye in a jar full of formaldehyde. Returning to the body, he placed the instrument against the remaining eye - and hesitated.

James glanced at the red feather in his hat band. Now dried from the fire, it stood upright, witnessing his indecision.

If he took both eyes, there would be nothing for Viola. She would insist on trying to incriminate him with her optograms. *There wasn't enough light.* Better he left one eye behind, to give her false hope. He placed the instrument back on the table beside him and picked up his autopsy knife.

James gathered his blood-stained clothes and overcoat. He twisted

them into a loose rope, as thick as his remaining wrist, and coiled them onto the fire grate along with the remnants of the rags he had used to clean his equipment. He redeemed a clean jacket from his bag, and slipped on a pair of new gloves.

He seized the wooden box on the dresser.

Locked.

James retrieved Mary's keys from his soiled jacket. The tumblers clicked as he turned the brass key in the lock.

Inside the box were two bundles of letters, each tied with a yellow ribbon. He flipped through them. One set contained correspondence with Doctor Williams. James slipped them into his coat pocket. The second bundle was from Mr Browne. James read them carefully, selecting one to add to the cache in his pocket. The rest were thrown onto the growing pile of refuse on the grate.

With Mary's folded clothes now placed on the end of the bed, James dropped her boots by the hearth, and tossed the opulent bonnet on top of the discard pile.

He had been working by lamplight since the fire had died over an hour ago. James grabbed one of the letters, twisted it tightly and poked it into the lamp's flame. A surge of heat rushed over his face as the paper burned. He prodded the pile in the grate, making sure the remaining letters caught fire.

The bonnet shifted under the draft as the flames grew. James caught it, plucked a red feather from the crown, nudged it back onto the fire, and placed a kettle on top to keep it secure. He pushed the second feather into the band of his hat.

James turned and dusted off his hands. He surveyed the room. Tomorrow's headlines should create acceptable horror and unrest. His employer could not fault him.

He donned his hat and a spare Inverness coat, and collected his bag. He peeked past the window curtain, into the courtyard. The rain had stopped but the cloud cover remained, obscuring the half-moon and strangling its light.

All was silent.

James locked the door behind him and pocketed the key. Now this saga was over, he could finally return to his research unhindered.

The carriage slowed and shuddered to a halt. Viola poked her head out of the carriage window. Through the drizzling rain, she saw several carriages waiting in line along Commercial Street.

A surging crowd pushed against one of the carriages before them. Men shouted. Several police constables linked their arms, attempting to provide a human barrier to prevent any carriages from entering Dorset Street.

The crowd soon pushed past them and swelled forward. The officers retreated along the street to regroup.

Viola felt a warm hand on her arm.

"Viola, please sit down. You could get hurt, if the carriage starts suddenly," pleaded Collins.

Viola hushed him. She leaned out further to get a better view of the road ahead.

"I can't see what's going on," she said.

A shatter of pottery rocked the carriage wall beside her, splashing a fine mist of ale over her face. A strong arm wrapped around her waist, pulling her back into the cab and out of harm's way.

"I told you this was not a good idea," Collins grumbled.

"The Inspector requested our presence," Viola replied. She pulled a lace-edged handkerchief from her purse and wiped her face. She screwed her nose up as she sniffed the linen.

Ugh, stale beer.

"I hazard he meant at the Station, not at the crime scene, and not in the middle of a growing riot," Collins said.

"Where is your sense of adventure, Doctor Collins?" Viola asked.

The carriage lurched forward, further into the crowd and turned into Dorset Street. The horses plodded on towards the scene of the murder. Damp bodies jostled the cab. Collins reached across and wrestled the window shut, muffling the din.

When their carriage reached Millers Court, Viola could see another chain of men blocking the entrance. Several officers wrestled back reporters who waved their notebooks in front of them. One man carried a large camera, pressing it hard against one of the officer's arms, in an effort to break the chain.

Viola jiggled on her seat, trying to get a better view of the fray through the closed window. A group of five officers marched on the reporters, pushing them back, creating a small clearing near the mouth of the lane way to Millers Court.

Viola knocked on the roof of the cab. Again the cab jerked as it came to a halt.

"Viola, I do not think this is one of your best ideas," said Collins.

"You would prefer I sit at home and do nothing but needlepoint?" replied Viola. "That would not be a challenge worthy of my education nor of your expectations. You would be bored with me within a month."

Her companion remained silent. Viola turned to him and winked.

"Come on, the rain is clearing."

Viola grabbed her parasol, jumped from the carriage and dashed up the laneway toward the waiting Constables. Collins took a deep breath and followed her out of the relative safety of the warm cab.

"Wait here," he instructed the driver. He pushed his way through the crowd of curious onlookers that folded in behind Viola's passage.

The Constable was polite, but insistent; "No one is to enter the courtyard.”

“But Inspector Abberline has requested my presence, as part of the investigation,” Viola explained politely.

The Constable did not look convinced. Viola rummaged in her bag and produced the letter of request. The constable frowned and called for one of the officers behind him. After a quick discussion, the second officer snatched the letter and retreated further down the lane way.

The officer returned in a few minutes. He shook his head as he passed a message to the Constable.

“The Inspector has returned to Whitechapel Station, Miss. I suggest your presence may be expected there,” said the Constable. He smiled, tipped his hat and returned his attentions to the rabble.

Viola turned to Collins.

“We can’t do anything here,” Collins said. “We’d better leave.”

“But they still have the letter,” replied Viola.

Collins’ reply was lost in the sound of the crowd, which out-rivalled that of the street sellers on High Street market day.

The reporter, who wielded the camera, had caught up to them and now jostled his way to the front of the throng. He pushed hard up against the line-up, almost knocking Viola off her feet.

She turned and lashed out at the ruffian, only to have her parasol stopped mid-air by a familiar hand. Collins smiled faintly at her, as he pushed the parasol away from his face.

“It is not safe to stay here, Viola. Maybe needlepoint would be a safer option?” he yelled, barely audible over the growing din.

“Not for you,” Viola cautioned. “It involves a sharp implement, and I have good aim.”

James strained to survey the spectators, now beginning to bristle in anger. Mr Browne, a few inches taller than James, had a better view of the growing throng. He leaned down and spoke quietly to James.

"Well done, Findlay." Mr Browne nodded in appreciation. "You may have been a little too enthusiastic, but efficient. It has had the desired effect. The Society will be pleased with the result. The crowd are definitely displeased with the establishment's ineffectualness. And now another unsolved murder." He grinned.

James shot him a dark glance.

"Come now, Findlay. Don't tell me you do not enjoy your work. I know you better than that, better than you think," he said.

James stared through the crowd as if they were ghosts. He visualised the alleyway beyond. He knew the horror that now confronted the Constabulary.

"You promised me funds for my research - research that will improve their lot, research that could save lives. The good of the many is worth the lives of a few... traitors," he replied.

Browne studied James for a moment. "Ah, altruism is such a noble vice."

Viola turned to Collins. He was preoccupied with distancing her from the angry mob. Her gaze flittered over the crowd. More onlookers were arriving, including those whose dress was more suited for a Sunday outing, more likely hailing from further afield.

Word had spread quickly. The Ripper had struck again.

Through the seething bodies, Viola spied a tall, moustachioed man wearing a well-cut grey suit, matching bowler hat and gloves. He carried a walking cane topped with a serpent head. A memory tugged at her consciousness, not quite willing to expose itself just yet.

Viola squinted, trying to get a better glimpse of the gentleman and his companion, with whom he conversed. She darted her head to improve her line of sight, then spied a hat with a red feather. Viola sucked in a sharp breath and leaned to the side in order to view the hat's owner. Her body trembled.

Findlay!

Their eyes locked for just a second. He blinked, and bolted like a rabbit fleeing its hunter. The Man in Grey watched James' hurried departure, and turned back to scan the area where Viola stood.

Viola stepped behind the photographer, out of Findlay's line of sight. She tilted her head, still trying to observe Findlays' companion.

"I saw him!" she said.

"Saw who?" Collins asked.

"Findlay," she replied.

"That is highly unlikely," replied Collins.

"I tell you, it was him. I would know him anywhere."

"It is your imagination."

"He was talking to a man in a grey suit." Viola searched for the grey bowler. "Over there." She pointed in the direction of the Man in Grey, barely visible amongst the sea of bobbing black, brown and grey bowlers.

There was something familiar about that hat...

The Man in Grey turned and stared back in Viola's direction. He froze. His eyes narrowed. He mouthed something inaudible and melted into the crowd, removing his hat as he did so.

"No!" Viola thrust her parasol into Collins' chest, hitched up her skirts and dashed after the Man in Grey.

"Wait, Viola," he yelled. He caught his breath and followed her into the swarm.

Viola pushed her way through the crowd and made her way westward, away from the main street. The crowd showed no sign of thinning. She

could just spy the bare head of her quarry, as it occasionally surfaced above the crowd. For once in her life, she was glad she was tall for her sex.

As her prize raced along Dorset Street, the crowd dwindled quickly allowing him faster movement. He continued along the now empty street, and darted north into an alleyway. His footsteps thudded on the cobblestones, growing fainter. Then nothing.

Viola was alone. Behind her, she could hear other hurried steps. Daylight did not necessarily offer protection here, in one of the most dangerous streets in London. She slowed her pace, regretting the relinquishment of her parasol.

The footfalls grew louder. As Viola neared the alleyway, her pursuer's pace quickened. Viola glanced nervously over her shoulder. To her relief it was her friend who tracked her, still brandishing her parasol. Collins frowned and called out to her to wait for him.

Viola turned to the alleyway. She took a few steps into the dimness, and hesitated. Though it had only just gone midday, the tenements which lined the narrow thoroughfare allowed no sun to touch the cobblestones. Their long shadows overlapped, creating ominous pockets of obscuration, capable of transforming quarry into hunter.

It would be prudent to heed her friend's warning, yet she took another tentative step, allowing the gloom to envelop her. With the warming sun denied ingress, a chill crept along her skin. The sounds of the crowd were now muffled. She froze, straining to catch any hint of what lay before her.

A faint metallic scrape?

A hand fell on her shoulder.

"Viola!" Collins scolded. He pulled her back into the light of Dorset Street. "It is reckless to run off on your own."

"I saw him."

"You are obsessed with that man," Collins replied. His gentle hands now held her arm. His voice was calm. "Leave it, Viola. It is an unhealthy fascination. We should return you home. You will catch cold in those wet clothes."

"Please believe me. I know he is responsible for these murders."

Viola searched his eyes for any hint of support. Collins continued to scan the alley before them. Lines deepened in his forehead. He grasped Viola's hand and ushered her out of the alley.

"It is not safe to pursue him by yourself. You need to trust in Inspector Abberline to do his job," said Collins.

"And you should trust me." Viola pursed her lips and snatched back her parasol.

Collins' jaw dropped. He opened his mouth. He blinked. He looked into her eye.

"I believe you think you saw him," Collins replied.

He slipped his arm around Viola's waist. Her heart skipped as a tingling warmth spread over her, warding off some of the chill. She took a deep breath and leaned into his shoulder, allowing him to manoeuvre her away from the alley and back towards the main street.

That's a start.

In the shadows, James waited. He remained hidden under the stairs that clung to the side of the tenement. He pressed his back against the brick wall. His gloved finger still lingered on his lips, cautioning Mr Browne to remain quiet. Mr Browne breathed heavily, having raced to catch up to James.

They had watched Viola edge towards their hiding place, had overheard the conversation, and her departure with Collins. Disappointed, James flicked his wrist. The knife slipped back into its hidden sheath, beneath his coat sleeve.

Unhealthy fascination...? James chuckled. *She is mine. Henry Collins will not have her.*

"That woman knows too much," Mr Browne whispered. "I have warned you before, about the company you keep."

James tugged on his cuffs and straightened his sleeves. "I think it's time to visit with an old friend."

The lone facade of Whitechapel Police Station towered between two converging cobblestoned roads, its wedged slabs of cream and red brick dulled under the overcast sky. The rain had finally cleared, leaving large pools of water in the cobblestone furrows and the dips in the uneven footpath.

Viola waited on the footpath across the road from the Station's main entrance. Collins paid the driver. As their carriage pulled away, Viola noticed a tall man in a grey suit emerge from the building. He unhooked his walking cane from his forearm; its serpent head stared at her with unblinking silver eyes. The man slipped a grey bowler on his head and scanned the street, as he stepped down onto the footpath.

Viola heard a splash as his boot landed in a puddle at the bottom of the step. The man grumbled and shook his boot. He glanced up at them, catching Viola's gaze. He had big bushy sideburns. Viola bit her lip.

There is something familiar...

The man squinted, still holding her gaze. A carriage rolled up to meet him. He broke eye contact and leaped into the carriage, signalling the driver to leave.

Viola tugged Collins' sleeve gently and nodded in the direction of the carriage.

"That man," she said.

"What man?" asked Collins.

"In the carriage there," she replied. "I think I recognise him. He was the man we chased this morning."

Collins squinted in the direction of the carriage.

"No, he doesn't have a moustache. And besides, why would he be visiting the Station?" Collins replied. "Everything doesn't have to be a conspiracy, Viola." He slipped his arm around hers and patted her hand. "Come on, you have work to do."

Viola watched as the carriage continued south along Commercial Street. She was sure the man was still watching her. She felt a gentle tug on her arm.

"Come on, we don't want to keep the Inspector waiting," said Collins.

Viola lifted her skirts as she tiptoed through the shallow puddle near the entrance of the Station. Collins followed her inside, remaining close by her side. She scanned the room. Marylebone could not boast such a large collection of soon-to-be-incarcerated miscreants during the day. Nor was it as bloated with prostitutes, even in the early hours of the morning. She found herself relieved that her friend had insisted on accompanying her.

The Desk Sergeant nodded as they approached his desk.

"We have an appointment with Inspector Abberline," said Viola.

The Sergeant motioned to a Constable, who led them down a corridor and through to the Inspector's Office.

An earthy aroma of truffles, toasted caramel and leather filled the room. Inspector Abberline waved away an errant wisp of smoke. A stack of papers sat on Abberline's desk. Around it were strewn newspapers and handwritten statements. Behind him sat a squat bookshelf full of scientific journals. A selection of clockwork devices and a set of miniature screwdrivers sat on the top shelf, next to a tin cigar box.

Abberline popped his pen into its inkwell, and tucked some notes into his journal. He snapped it shut and secured it tightly with a cord.

"Thank you for coming," he said. He motioned to the tea tray on his desk, with a fresh pot of tea and china cups. "Perfect timing. It should still be hot."

"Excellent," replied Collins. He licked his lips. He cast his gaze over the tray.

Viola remained silent. She was displeased she had been dismissed from Dorset Street, only to be summoned to Whitechapel Station the very same afternoon. If she had been a man...

"I am glad you accepted our invitation, Mrs Stewart," Abberline began.

"Doctor," Viola corrected.

Abberline raised an eyebrow and glanced at Collins.

"She does have a doctorate in optics," he replied, with a smirk.

"I must apologise, Doctor Stewart." The Inspector cleared his throat and shifted in his seat. "You know, I wanted to be an engineer. Not everyone can get what they desire, eh?"

Viola studied him. *He dresses like a banker; surely his family had money?*

"And why didn't you, Inspector?" she asked.

Abberline blinked.

"Um..." He straightened some papers beside him. "Circumstances change," he said.

Viola relaxed her shoulders. *Perhaps he understands? Perhaps he would listen?*

Viola cleared her throat.

"Why have you not arrested Findlay?" Viola asked. "He is our murderer."

"I have interviewed the doctor." Abberline sighed and interlaced his fingers, then leaned his elbows on his desk. "He has an alibi for the nights in question. A Mr Grey vouched for him."

"The same Mr Grey whom I saw leaving, just now?" asked Viola.

"The man all dressed in grey and sporting a fine set of sideburns?"

Abberline nodded.

"Then you may want to interview him again," said Viola.

Collins took a deep breath and pinched the bridge of his nose. A faint grimace clung to his lips.

"Why do you think this is advisable, Doctor Stewart?" asked Abberline.

"He was at the murder scene this morning, in the company of James Findlay. They ran when I saw them together."

Abberline turned to Collins, who responded with a slight shrug. Abberline placed his nib pen back onto the table beside his notebook and leaned back into his chair.

"I followed him down Dorset Street, but he escaped," said Viola.

Collins nodded.

Viola took a slow breath, watching the interaction between the two men as she continued.

"I am not prone to flights of fancy, Inspector Abberline."

"Of that, I am sure, Doctor Stewart, but don't you think that a little reckless, if he was involved?" replied Abberline. "You have seen what the Whitechapel Murderer does to women on the street."

Viola pursed her lips and narrowed her eye.

"Do you think I look like a prostitute?" she said.

Abberline opened his mouth but did not speak. He shot a glance at Collins, who arched an eyebrow. Collins' fingers smoothed down his moustache, not quite obscuring his smile. He raised his hand, palm-forward, and shook his head faintly. Abberline swallowed and addressed Viola:

"I did not mean to imply any disrespect. Dorset Street does not carry its bad reputation without reason. It is a very dangerous area. You were lucky to have an escort."

"Doctor Stewart would not go off on a whim," replied Collins.

Viola grinned. *He believes me.*

"I apologise, Doctor Stewart," said Abberline. "I do hope this will not change your mind about performing an optogram? It could provide valuable information for the investigation. I think scientific methods are well suited for such cases and may well be the future of investigation."

"Apology accepted," said Viola. She glanced at the paraphernalia in his bookshelf. "As a fellow scientist I know the value of facts. Can you tell me more about Mr Grey's statement?" she asked.

Abberline rubbed his chin and sighed.

"I can't see any harm in your knowing," he said. "On the night of the Marylebone murder, Findlay was attending a Research Meeting in Marylebone. So that explains your chance meeting."

Abberline leaned back in his chair and reached for his cup of tea.

Viola sucked in a short breath, then smiled wryly.

"A Research Meeting, in Marylebone?"

"Yes, I have a signed statement from Mr Grey," Abberline replied.

Viola placed her bag on the table and produced a sealed letter from within its depths.

"You may want to reconsider that alibi, Inspector. *This* is a signed statement, from Sir Archibald Huntington-Smythe of Harley Street, testifying that both he and Mr Grey attended the meeting in question. Mr Findlay did not attend. So, I doubt if your Mr Grey can vouch for where Mr Findlay was." Viola slid the missive across the table. "You have heard of Sir Archibald Huntington-Smythe?"

"The mechanical limb doctor?"

"That is he. I doubt that he would be prone to fanciful conjecture or falsifying witness statements. Can the same be said of Mr Grey?" said Viola.

Abberline read the statement. He frowned.

"*If* he is our man," he replied finally, "we have no other evidence. We employed bloodhounds after the last month's murder. There was nothing to link Findlay or his clinic to the murder." Abberline folded up the statement and slipped it inside his notebook. "I will send a Constable to bring him in for a further interview and have my Sergeant organise a search of his clinic."

Viola latched her bag and smiled.

"Then I should get to work on providing you with some scientific proof," she said.

"Thank you, Doctor Stewart. My men have set up your equipment, as instructed."

"We shall see," said Viola.

Viola had been provided with a room on the second level at the rear of the Station. It was small, and looked suspiciously like a hastily converted storeroom, but was suitable for her needs. Viola would have preferred to have worked at Marylebone but the Inspector had insisted on not letting any evidence out of his jurisdiction.

Shuttered windows blocked the daylight. Red filters covered each lamp, casting long, dark shadows into the corners of the room.

"I wouldn't be surprised if there were spiders hiding in the shadows," she said.

"Or rats?" replied Collins. His eyes gleamed.

Viola rolled up her sleeves, her arms pale under the filtered light. She slipped on a pair of leather half-sleeves, and pulled them up to cover her forearms. She adjusted her magnifying spectacles, flicking several small filtered lenses in front of her left eye, until she maximised her vision under the rubied cast of the room's lighting.

Collins re-positioned one of the red-filtered lamps to reduce the shadows on the bench. Beside one lamp sat a rectangular metal box. A fan was encased in a metal cage at one end of the contraption. A large round filter was bolted to the opposite end.

Collins turned the small metal wheel on the side of the box. The fan spun irregularly, drawing away the fumes that wafted up from a metal photographic tray filled with Potassic Alum.

Viola examined the eye in her hand. The cornea was already starting to cloud, reducing the vibrance of its once sapphire coloured iris. The Ripper had taken its counterpart as a trophy; there was no allowance for mistakes nor to confirm the result. Any further delay could prove disastrous.

"We only get one chance at this," she said.

Viola took a deep breath and pushed the fine knife into the eyeball. A viscous liquid oozed from the cut, forming a large gelatinous bead before collapsing. It then cascaded outside the sclera and over the orbit.

Viola grimaced as she forced the knife in deeper. With a gentle sawing motion, she sliced along the equator, then removed the rear half of the orbit. She laid it on a glass plate, pinned the edges down carefully so the retina would remain flat, and lowered it into the tray's solution.

She looked up at Collins through the magnifying spectacles, and grinned. The most challenging part of the procedure was successfully completed; the retina was intact.

"And now we wait," she said.

Collins opened the shutters to allow more light into the small room.

Viola leaned closer to the chemical baths. The Alum fumes drifted, making her head spin.

Collins opened the door to aerate the stuffy room.

"Are you unwell, Viola?" asked Collins.

She nodded and waved him away.

"Let's see what we have here," she said.

Viola meticulously lifted the fixed tissue from the liquid-filled tray. She gently blotted it with cotton gauze, carefully lowered another glass plate on top, and sealed it with a wooden frame.

"It looks like a photographic plate," said Collins.

"Yes," replied Viola. She noted the irony. *Me, dabbling in photography!*

She held up the large glass slide and manoeuvred it, trying to catch the light from the unshuttered window. The light from the setting sun was unsatisfactory. She moved towards the wall lighting.

"Can you make it brighter?" she asked.

Collins removed the red glass that covered the lamp and turned up the gas. Viola peered through the thick-lensed spectacles and grumbled. She passed the plate and magnifying spectacles to Collins. He scrutinised the optogram. He tilted it one way, then another. He frowned and met Viola's gaze. His brilliant blue eyes filled the entire lens, both comical and endearing.

"Nothing?" he asked.

"Nothing," she replied.

"We failed?"

"We did not fail," said Viola, "because there is no bleaching of the Visual Purple, at all. I can only conclude there was not enough light to create any image. Miss Kelly was dead before sunrise," said Viola.

"That agrees with the coroner's assessment," admitted Abberline. His nose crinkled as he entered the room.

"You could have mentioned this earlier," Viola grumbled. "There was little chance of any success, in such low light levels." She handed the glass plate to Abberline.

"We had to be sure," Abberline replied. "There was a great deal of evidence burnt in the grate. We had hoped there may have been enough light."

Viola's eye widened.

"You know how an optogram works?" she asked.

"I did some reading on the subject after our last meeting," Abberline replied. "I need all the help I can get on this investigation, Doctor Stewart. There have been some interesting journal articles on using finger prints to identify suspects. If a Frenchman can do it, then we can. I've had the constables searching for finger prints in Kelly's room."

"Finger prints?" asked Collins.

"The skin on the tip of a finger has ridges, which form individual patterns, yes?" said Abberline.

Collins ran his thumb over his fingers.

"If we can record any marks left behind, they can be matched to an individual," continued Abberline.

"Have you finger printed Findlay?" asked Viola.

The Inspector cleared his throat. "Unfortunately, we are having difficulties ascertaining his current whereabouts. No one has seen him at the Hospital or the Workhouse. He's nowhere to be found."

"Have you checked his clinic?" asked Collins.

"Yes, the constables have searched there. They found nothing."

"Does that not confirm his guilt, Inspector Abberline?" asked Viola. "He knows you are searching for him,"

"Not necessarily, Doctor Stewart. There was nothing to connect him to the murders."

Viola cleared her throat.

"Yes, you did see him with a suspicious character, and he has no alibi, but we still need more proof," replied Abberline. He flipped open his notebook and placed it on the work bench. "Doctors do not keep regular hours, as you know. However, I do have men watching the clinic, in case he returns."

"I suppose you could be correct," said Viola. She nodded and cast her eye over his notebook. Fortuitously he had neat writing, allowing it to be legible enough to be read, even in the red lighting.

Viola remembered the blood red feather she had made for her bonnet, the one she was going to give Donell. *The one Findlay stole.* She swallowed. Edinburgh was a long time ago. A decade past.

But only he holds the answer to what happened to Anne.

Viola mentally noted the clinic's address.

"I must be off, gentlemen. It is getting late. I will meet with you here in the morning."

"I thought we could have supper," said Collins. His gaze fell to the notebook on the table. He rolled his eyes.

Viola yawned and patted her lips.

"I am too fatigued. I think I will take a cab directly home," she said. She collected her gloves and bag. "Good evening, gentlemen."

A crisp breeze greeted Viola as she stepped out of Whitechapel Police Station. She pulled her *visite* snugly around her neck. The air was thick, held captive by the persisting clouds, closing the night around her.

Viola searched for any cheery light from the half-moon.

At least there won't be much fog tonight.

She skipped over the puddle near the bottom step and hailed a passing hansom cab. *Appearances must be upheld.* She was certain Collins would be watching to ensure her safe departure.

The cab pulled up to the curb. Viola climbed into the seat, and glanced back towards the Station. There was no sign of Collins.

"Church Street," she instructed the driver. *Quickly, before he catches up.*

The cab turned the corner along Commercial Street, out of direct line-of-sight of the Police Station. Viola rummaged in her bag for her newly-fashioned tinted spectacles. They would not look out of place in Spitalfields. Many of the gentry and upper classes wore them when they

went slumming, as they provided a small measure of anonymity.

Viola had specially adapted them, to afford an extra advantage. She removed her eye patch, slipped on the spectacles, and tilted her head from side to side. The reflections in the prismed mirrors, concealed in the side-shields, proved very effective in compensating for the lack of vision on her right side.

She glanced out of the window behind the cab. She was not being followed.

"Church Street, Miss," announced the driver. The cab shook as it stopped.

Viola slipped out of the cab and paid the driver. It would not take long to reach Findlay's clinic by foot. She made her way past a small group of devout church-goers who cast only a fleeting glance in her direction, shook their heads and continued in their piety.

Viola turned her head to inspect the augmented peripheral vision of her creation in the lower light levels of the secondary thoroughfare. However, the double-silvered mirrors were proving less satisfactory the further she ventured from reliable lighting.

Viola's shoe rolled on a loose cobblestone. She sighed. She continued on towards the address in Abberline's notebook.

Shadows passed through her vision, as their owners made their way to and from the Ten Bells. One shadow seemed to be more persistent than the others. It hovered, just beyond recognition. Always there.

There was a tink of metal on cobblestones.

Viola quickened her pace. The further she travelled from the Ten Bells, the fewer locals passed by. She turned into a side lane, nudging the last street lamp on Church Street as she passed by. The added field of view was still no cure for poor depth perception.

Concentrate.

Viola glanced behind her. Still the shadow remained. If she made her way back to Commercial Street now, there would be the anonymity of larger crowds and the relative safety of more substantial street lighting.

I can't go back the way I came.

The lane was dark and narrow. Overlapping footsteps echoed, reverberating off the brick buildings around her, making it difficult to determine if they were her own or that of the shadowy figure behind her. Another tink.

Viola's heart raced. She squinted and searched the silvered glass that edged her spectacles. There were two shadows now, outlined in the faint lamp light that flickered at the intersection behind her.

Viola reached into the pocket beneath her skirts. Her fingers curled around a small metal object; she put it to her lips, wincing as the piercing trill vibrated uncomfortably on her ear drums.

The two figures behind her froze for a moment, and sprinted in her direction. Through the ringing in her ears, she could hear other footsteps converging on where she stood. The shadows' owners would reach her first.

Please do not let it be Findlay.

The shadows behind her grew larger.

Viola lost her nerve. She screamed and bolted down an alley way towards the soft glow that bathed Commercial Street, leaving her pursuers in the street behind her.

"Where did she go?" asked one of the men.

"Enough games," James mumbled.

He tapped the metal tip of his walking cane onto the cobblestones and scanned the shadowed street. He, too, could hear the rallying footfalls. A second policeman's whistle sounded.

"I hope she's safe," said the man. "That's another policeman's whistle. We need to be on the lookout. It's not safe around here."

James ran a hand over his moustache, and pulled his billy-cock hat down over his eyes.

"I have an urgent appointment. I need to go," said James.

"But you ain't got your bag, Doctor Jack," said the man.

James froze. Doctor Jack was the name given to him by those he attended in the workhouse. He had been recognised.

James turned around slowly. They were still alone. He slipped his arm around the man's shoulders. "I think she was frightened and ran down the laneway. Poor thing. We should make sure she is safe, what with the Ripper still on the loose," he said.

The man nodded and peered down the darkened lane.

"She might need a doctor," said James.

The man allowed himself to be led further into the darkness where *Jack* could begin his work.

There was a faint clicking, then a swish. The knife found its home between the taller man's ribs. Jack supported the body as it grew limp. He let it slide quietly onto the cobblestones.

No witnesses.

He shot a furtive glance back along the laneway. The policeman's whistle trilled once more.

Closer.

This time, it was just beyond the end of the alley.

Too close.

He slid into a narrow alley between the buildings and hurried eastwards towards the Ten Bells' back entrance. He could rely on the barkeep's taciturnity.

Chapter 3: Conspiracies

Doctor Henry Collins sat on the stone step of Viola's Marylebone terrace house, almost hidden by the shadows in the small entry alcove. He stared out into the street, scanning each adjoining thoroughfare for any sign of movement. No movement. He cocked his head, straining to hear. The occasional muffled clop of hooves skimmed the edges of his hearing, but came no nearer.

Where are you, Viola?

He had seen Findlay's address in the Inspector's notebook, had been suspicious of Viola's sudden departure. He had rushed after her, only to see her carriage turn towards the clinic.

Henry pinched the bridge of his nose and massaged his forehead.

Too slow, too slow.

He had made his way quickly to Findlay's Clinic. There had been no sign of her. In desperation, he raced back to Marylebone, hoping to find Viola safely ensconced at home, waylaying his suspicions she had renewed her solo investigative efforts. His hopes had been thwarted.

How could she be so reckless?

She blamed Findlay for Anne's disappearance and seemed determined to condemn him for it. He had become her personal tormentor. She would not give in until he was caught.

Or worse...

I shouldn't have let you leave alone. Why didn't I listen? If it had been Donell, I would have never questioned the Man in Grey's existence.

I would have jumped at the chance to share in an adventure.

With each minute, his anger at Viola's recklessness faltered, giving way to anxiety. Each swell of panic would be met with a vague rationale heralding hope. As the surrounding sounds of the night's activity waned, he was left to his silent brooding.

Next time, I will listen. I will support you and damn convention.

After hours of waiting, the night chill had seeped into his bones. His joints refused to move, making it more difficult to fight the somnolence that washed over him in waves.

He stared into the street, his chin balanced precariously on the ball of his hand. The cobblestones blurred. The street lamp seemed to slip sideways, spawning a twin. The light began to fade...

A hansom cab rattled along the street, slowing as it neared.

Henry shook his head and jumped to his feet. He swallowed, forcing his heart to retreat back into his chest. It pounded fiercely in defiance, refusing to be controlled. He squinted, bobbing his head as he tried to discern the cab's occupant.

As the cab passed under the street lamp, Henry saw a grey-gloved hand grasped the window frame. The rim of a grey bowler emerged from the cabin's shadow. The gloved hand tapped on the side of the carriage. The driver flicked the reigns. The carriage jolted and hastened off along the street.

Now you have me seeing conspiracies, Viola.

Henry collapsed onto the top step and leaned back into the shadows. He could hear faint sounds of the scullery staff finishing up their late night tasks. The whistle of wind raced up the step, danced around his body and clawed at his hair. He could feel the tick of his pocket watch as it marked time. With each tick the warmth faded, his hope drained, until he felt nothing but numbness.

Another wave of lethargy engulfed him. His head lolled, causing his elbow to slip from his knee, waking him with a start. His gaze darted

around the portico and along the street. Still no sign of his wayward oculist.

Henry buried his head in his hands and sighed. All too often, in his work, he had seen the results of lone travellers waylaid on the dark streets. He remembered the eyeless body he had autopsied. The face faded. He imagined Viola's cold body laid out on the marble table, her skin pale, her one eye clouded.

Henry drew a sharp breath, wincing as the cold air filled his lungs. He rubbed his eyes, trying to rid himself of the image and fought the tears, which threatened to take control.

Please come home, Viola.

Another carriage bounced over the uneven cobble stones. The clatter of horse hooves grew louder. He dropped his hands from his face and lifted his eyes to peer through his numb fingers. Swirling blood echoed in his ears. His heart raced. He held his breath and struggled to slow his breathing.

The see-sawing adrenaline had exhausted him. This carriage, like those before it, would continue ferrying its passenger past his vigil and safely to their own home. Henry closed his eyes and squeezed them tightly.

A hansom cab rattled along the street toward him. Its wheel skittered against the gutter as it stopped in front of him. A soft footstep landed on the nearby flagstones. There was a murmur, followed by hurried footfalls. Heeled boots clicked on the stone steps.

Silk skirts caressed his hand. A soft hand brushed past his face.

Viola shrieked and jumped back down the step. Her parasol snapped open between them, its sharp point ready to find its mark.

Henry opened his eyes. Before him stood a dishevelled-looking Viola.

"Viola! Thank goodness," said Henry.

Henry rose and moved into the lamp light. His face was drained of colour, his breathing shallow.

"Henry George Collins!" Viola scowled. "How dare you frighten me in such a manner."

"Where have you been, Viola?" he asked quietly.

"None of your business." She snapped the parasol shut, climbed the stairs and fumbled in her bag.

"Are you...?" Henry swallowed. "Are you well?"

"Of course I am well. Why wouldn't I be?"

"I've been worried. I saw the entry in the Inspector's notebook. You went to find Findlay, didn't you?"

Viola remained silent. Henry stepped closer.

"I took a cab to his clinic. You were not there," he said.

"You followed me? Am I a child? A true friend would trust my judgement." Viola's hand shook as she rammed the door key into the lock.

"And if I had insisted on helping you, you would have scolded me. I could not let you go into danger alone. You vex me, Viola!"

"I know what I am doing. I can look after myself," she snapped. She ran her gaze over Henry's crumpled attire. "I can't say the same for you."

Henry opened his mouth. He was too exhausted to reply. Every muscle in his body ached. He had experienced more emotional upheaval than any gentleman should have to endure in a single day. He was both angry at her recklessness and relieved that his worst fears had proved false. There was no energy left to fight; all his effort was concentrated on restraining himself from taking her in his arms, and never letting go.

The door latch clicked loudly in the uncomfortable silence.

"It is getting late, please let us not argue," he sighed.

"Then we should say goodnight, Doctor Collins. And you can offer your apologies at a more opportune time. Right now I need a stiff drink and a warm fire."

Most women would never leave the safety of the hearth. *But not my Viola.*

There was fire in her eyes. The same fire that had ensnared him so long ago; the fire that threatened to consume him. She was the fire, he was the moth. Too long he had fluttered helplessly around the edges of her glow.

Henry licked his lips. He couldn't part, allowing her to think ill of him.

"I heard police whistles. Viola, I thought they may have been for you," he whispered.

Viola stood motionless, her hand still holding the key in the lock, as if frozen in time. The faint gong of the hall clock reached them. Three o'clock.

She pushed the door open, entered and turned to face Henry. She still wore her tinted spectacles. Faint silvery scars crept towards her eyebrow and across her right cheek, just visible beyond the tinted lens. A tear trickled down her face.

"The whistles *were* for me, Henry," she whispered.

Henry caught his breath, willing his heart to restart beating. He stepped into the entry hall, away from prying eyes.

His hands shook as reached up and gently removed her spectacles. He looked into her green eye. Her pupil twitched, causing the surrounding small flecks of gold to dance and gleam in the lamplight. He saw only her beauty, her spirit. He traced scars that ran down to her empty socket, and gently wiped the tears from her cheek.

Viola gasped and slammed the door shut behind them. She fumbled in her bag for her eyepatch. The pink-laced confection dropped to the tiled floor. She clasped her hand over her eye.

"Please, don't look," she pleaded.

Henry touched her hand, traced his finger along hers and gently lifted them away from her eye. He retrieved the eye patch, slid it over her soft, dark curls and covered the injured orbit.

"If you wish." He kissed her hand gently and looked her directly in the eye. "Just please tell me I have not lost you, Viola."

Viola could feel the tears return. She blinked to clear her vision, and looked into Henry's eyes. Their brilliance had dulled a little. Viola's heart ached.

Have I done this to you?

Etiquette decreed it was impolite to stare a man in the eye but Viola did not look away. She held his gaze.

I could fall into those blue eyes and be adrift forever.

"Don't leave me alone, Henry," she whispered.

Henry's eyes widened. He gulped. "You can't mean that."

Viola smiled, realising his misunderstanding.

"I will have Polly make you up the spare room. Tomorrow you will accompany me to the clinic to investigate," Viola replied.

Viola could feel the tension slip from Henry's fingers. His eyes glinted.

"Tell me about these Men in Grey?" he asked.

Viola strained to hear the conversation. She heard only snippets, though Henry was barely ten feet from her. Through the lingering fog, the doctor's sensible dark grey coat blended into the dingy surroundings, almost indistinguishable from the buildings around them. He pointed into the fog and mouthed something. The guttersnipe shook his head. Henry's shoulders slumped. He pressed a coin into the boy's hand. Then the boy was gone.

Henry led her through the narrow lanes of Whitechapel in search of Findlay's private clinic. Viola's pale pink skirts stood out from under her *visite*, like a bright flame in the thick morning mist, drawing the attention of the denizens that skulked there. Henry had accompanied her to the East End as he had promised, though he had not neglected to remark on her choice of attire.

What does he know?

A cold gust of air whistled through the laneway. Viola's coat flapped open. She shivered. Henry slipped off his wool coat.

"No, you don't," said Viola. She tugged on her *visite*, wrapping it around her chest and securing the buttons. *Or I'll never hear the end of it.*

"Did the boy know the address?" Viola asked.

"No," Henry replied.

From the murky depths of the alley behind them there was a loud crash, and a clatter. Someone cursed.

Two shadowy figures bobbed in the fog ahead.

Viola slipped her arm around Henry's. He put his hand on hers and ushered her along the lane toward the relative safety of the High Street.

"Perhaps we missed a turn?" said Henry.

"This was the address in the Inspector's notebook. Findlay said he had rooms around here," said Viola.

The figures strolled closer, revealing themselves to be two men.

Henry pulled Viola closer.

"He must have lied about the clinic. I doubt if he even cares about these people. His mother insisted he take up medicine, did you know that?" said Henry.

One of the men stopped and tipped his hat.

"Are you looking for Doctor Jack?" he asked. The man grinned, revealing a lack of dental hygiene, and several teeth.

Viola gasped. She tightened her grip on Henry's arm.

"Jack?" repeated Viola. *Jack - the nickname given to The Whitechapel Murderer.*

"We are looking for Doctor Findlay's private clinic," said Henry.

"I can help you," the man replied. His voice was hoarse, his appearance rough and he smelt of gin. "Most 'round here know him as Doctor Jack. He does free doctoring to those who need it."

Henry's brow wrinkled.

"I can show you where it is," said the man, "for a price."

Henry glanced at Viola. She nodded, and took a deep breath, regretting it as soon as the stale gin filled her nostrils.

I need to find him. I need to know the truth about Anne.

"Money first," replied the man.

He held out a grubby hand clothed in a tatty glove. Henry dropped a coin into his palm. The man snatched the coin and shoved it in his pocket.

"Follow me," he said.

He led them further into the fog, through a maze of lanes and alleys and stopped at an unadorned door, in dire need of repainting. He pointed at the brick building.

Viola eyed the man.

"Are you sure?" she asked.

The man nodded. "I sometimes deliver supplies to his rooms."

Henry dipped his head, trying to peer through the front window. His moustache twitched.

"Be a good man and fetch Inspector Abberline from Whitechapel Station. I will pay you handsomely on your return."

The man looked him in the eye and raised an eyebrow. He thrust out his empty hand and rubbed his thumb and forefinger together.

"Here." Henry placed a shilling in his hand. "I will pay you twice that if you fetch him immediately."

The man's fingers curled tightly around the coin. He tipped his hat and skittered off down a side alley.

Henry stepped closer to the smudged window. He peeked through a slit in the curtain.

"I do not think he's in residence," he said.

Viola grabbed the door handle. It jiggled in her hand, refusing to turn.

That would have been too easy.

Henry joined her on the low step. He motioned behind him, with a quick jerk of his head.

"Keep watch," he said.

Viola turned and scanned the street. The sun was almost directly above them. The long shadows had receded back towards the walls. Only a fine wisp of mist lingered now. The street was deserted.

The handle rattled behind her. There was a loud click. Viola turned to face Henry. He stood in the open doorway, grinning.

Viola stared at him.

"How did you...?"

"With all of your detecting, I had to find a way to keep up with you," he replied. He folded up a small roll of tools and pocketed them.

"You will have to show me how to do that," she insisted.

"I am not entirely sure that is a wise decision," he replied. "Besides, I need you to have a reason not to leave me behind next time you run off on one of your quests."

Viola followed Henry into the small, dank room. It was sparse; its only furniture was a bench, a small locked cupboard, and a small desk with a plain wooden chair. A fine layer of grime coated the walls and windows, being thicker near the small coal fire.

"He may be many things, including a murderer, but he wouldn't experiment in this filth," she said.

Henry surveyed the room.

"Agreed. His rooms were always overly neat at University," replied

Henry. "Donell used to badger him about it."

"We need to find his laboratory," said Viola.

Henry nodded and busied himself with searching the walls and stamping his foot on the floor boards, occasionally stealing a glimpse in Viola's direction.

Viola sat at the desk, searching each drawer thoroughly. Her hand slipped under the desk. Her finger knocked up against something. She smiled.

They did not need to wait long for the Constabulary to arrive.

Viola glanced up from her discovery as the portly figure of Inspector Abberline stormed through the door, followed by two Constables. Abberline doffed his hat briefly in her direction and ran his fingers over his chin making his bushy side whiskers bounce slightly.

"Morning, doctors," said Abberline. He scanned the room. "What is so urgent?"

"Findlay's hidden secrets," replied Viola.

She slipped her hand under the desk and pushed the button. There was a click, followed by a continuous ratcheting within the wall, which slowly ascended towards them. She rose from the chair, straightened her skirts and pursed her lips.

Henry dragged the chair from behind the desk.

Abberline placed his palm on the wall behind Viola. He slid his hand a few inches lower. His eyes widened.

"It's in the bloody wall," he said.

"Actually, I think it's beneath us," Henry replied.

Abberline pressed his ear against the panelled wall and knocked. He grinned, pressed one of the panels and stood back. A door-sized section slid aside to reveal a small room. It was bare, its only adornment a small brass lever attached to one side wall.

Abberline's eyes narrowed. He glared at the Constables.

"Why didn't you find this earlier, Smith?" he asked.

Constable Smith shrugged in reply.

"It's an Ascension Chamber," Abberline explained.

Viola peered into the cupboard-sized box.

"It looks like only four of us will fit in there, and that will be a squeeze," she said.

"Taylor, you're with me. You stay here, Smith," instructed Abberline. "See what else you missed."

Smith nodded.

Abberline stepped into the chamber; the floor shuddered under his weight. Taylor hesitated. He inspected the edge of the doorway, before gingerly stepping onto the floor.

Viola and Henry exchanged fleeting glances. It would be a tighter squeeze than anticipated.

Henry followed Taylor into the chamber, placing his body between Viola and the other men. He turned and offered his hand to Viola and drew her into the confined space, next to him.

Abberline grabbed the brass lever on the wall and pushed it downward. The door slid behind Viola, snagging her bustle. She jumped forward and whipped her hand behind her to free her skirts. The door snapped shut, cutting off all light. The Chamber descended.

Viola could feel Henry's body pressed against hers, his breath on her neck. The heat rose and settled into her cheeks.

She leaned onto the door behind her, in an effort to keep propriety to a maximum and body contact to a minimum. A handle jabbed into the back of her corset.

She drew a quiet breath, trying to fill her lungs and clear her head. Henry's scent filled her nostrils. Her heart fluttered.

Why was it taking so long!

The Ascension Chamber convulsed and clattered to a stop. The door remained closed. The blackness remained. Viola felt Henry lean closer, reaching around her body. His arm nudged gently against her waist, as he patted the door. Viola swallowed. He grabbed the handle and wrenched it downward. The chamber jerked.

Viola stumbled backwards as the door opened outward behind her. Her nostrils were the first to complain as they were assaulted by the pungent stench of formaldehyde and bleach. Viola was familiar with such odours, having assisted Henry in the morgue. This was beyond comparison. But neither masked the musty, mouldy smell of the damp cellar.

Her stomach was the next to complain, churning most inconveniently and expelling acidic lumps up her oesophagus. Viola clenched her teeth and swallowed the wave of nausea that followed. She snatched a handkerchief from her bag and covered her nose and mouth.

A trickle of light spilt into the cellar via a sliver of window left unboarded at the south end of the room.

Abberline followed Henry into the room.

"Disgusting," grumbled Abberline.

Viola ran her hand along the wall beside them. Logically there should be a light source nearby. Her finger thumped against a small toggle. She flicked it. The room filled with light.

"Electric light!" gasped the Constable.

"How could a workhouse doctor afford electricity?" asked Abberline.

"Findlay mentioned a rich benefactor who funds his research," replied Henry.

"I shall have to have a chat with this benefactor," said Abberline.

Viola heard a trickling sound. She pressed her ear against the bricked wall near the Ascension Chamber.

"Can you hear that?" she asked.

A hissing sound echoed through the Chamber, followed by a grating above its roof. A loud crack echoed further up the shaft, quickly followed by a whipping sound. The chamber shuddered.

Henry peered inside. He shook his head.

"It appears we will be here longer than expected," he said. "The cable has smashed through the roof of the Chamber. We won't be returning that way."

He jumped back into the cellar as the Ascension Chamber door slammed shut, silencing the ominous sounds.

Taylor tested the door's handle. It rattled impotently in his hand.

"It is locked, sir," he said.

"Bloody hell," yelled Abberline.

He strode toward the large metal table that dominated the centre of the room. Several medical tools lay neatly on one end. He shook his head and took a deep breath, coughing as the putrid smell filled his lungs.

"See what you can make of this, Collins," he said. He turned to the Constable. "Find us another exit, Taylor."

Viola glanced across the room. Diagrams, sketches and photographs papered the wall, spilling onto a cluttered wooden bench. Abberline had already taken an interest in the documents.

She wandered over to the west wall. Bottles of organs lay on the shelves that lined it. Various diagrams were pinned to the shelf edges. Under the paper curtain was a long bench brimming with equipment, contraptions and notebooks. Everything was arranged neatly in rows.

She lifted one of the contraptions, an articulated metal arm complete with working hand. The joints showed signs of wear. Nestled against the forearm was the upended skeleton of a bronze sheath. The broken remains of a sprung hinge were mounted to the wrist.

Viola replaced the mechanical on the bench. Compared to Sir Archibald's commissioned mechanicals, it was crude. This was not some vanity for High Society. It was practical.

She bit her lip. *What are you up to?*

A bottle of preserved eyes stared at her. Viola studied them. They were all green.

How odd.

Loose notes peeked out from under the jar. Viola pulled them out and turned the bottle to face away from her. Each eyeball bounced gaily in the preserving fluid and spun slowly back to face her. Viola grimaced. She dropped her handkerchief over the jar and turned to face the room.

She sifted through the loose pages; there were rough notes on initial eye transplant experiments, some of which showed promise. She flipped to the last of the pages, to a sketch of...

Her hand trembled. The blood chilled in her veins. The air closed in around her. It squeezed, making it impossible to breathe. The world blurred, as if behind frosted glass. Sounds faded. Even the stench receded.

The notes slipped from her hand and fluttered to the floor. Only the sketch remained. She was staring at her own image.

There was silence.

A shadow flitted beside her, trying to attract her attention. It would not desist. A gentle hand touched her forearm. The sketch was extricated from her numb fingers and disappeared from view.

The smell of formaldehyde returned to her nostrils, lifting the fog that enveloped Viola. Abberline's voice mumbled nearby.

The hand remained on her arm.

A voice buzzed in her ear, whispering something unintelligible. Viola shook her head, resisting the pull back to reality. The voice spoke again; the buzz was gone, the tone now more soothing.

"... we will find him, Viola. I will not leave your side until we do, until you are safe."

Henry's voice flowed like honey, sweet and comforting. Her blood thawed, returning the warmth to Viola's fingers and cheeks. The pressure on her chest eased. She took a deep breath and slipped her hand into his.

"I will keep you to your promise Henry Collins," she whispered.

"I found another door, sir!" announced Taylor.

"Excellent work, Constable. Once we get out of here, I will send for more men to collect all of this..." His nose wrinkled as he looked around them, "... evidence. Then you and Smith will find this wretched *Doctor Jack*."

"I, for one, will be glad to get out of here," said Henry.

"Ladies first," smiled Abberline. Taylor opened the door and stood aside. Viola composed herself and readied for her return to the structured society above. She stepped through the doorway. And screamed.

The foul odour rolled over her in waves, growing stronger with every intake of breath. Compared to the fetor in the cellar, this stench was one-hundred fold. This was no exit; it was a room full of foul experimentations, the sickly sweet odour of stale blood and an overpowering smell of brine.

Viola regretted relinquishing her protective handkerchief to such innocuous minutiae as inanimate eyeballs. She clasped her hand over her mouth and bent over, in a desperate attempt to regain control of her stomach.

The three men appeared simultaneously at the threshold of the room. Their faces contorted as they absorbed the horrors before them.

A low gurgling filled the room, broken only by an intermittent hissing sound. Small puffs of steam rose from behind the hideous contraption before them. Transparent hoses fed thick red liquid from large wooden barrels behind the wood-capped cylinder of glass. Vile yellow chemicals liquefied the saline and whole blood, providing sustenance to the headless torso which occupied the cylinder and kept the torso suspended in its unnatural state.

They watched in silence, unable to wrench their eyes from the horror, as its chest rose and fell with the beating of an unseen heart.

Viola heard retching from outside the room. Taylor had retreated back into the cellar. She closed her eye, wishing she had never seen the nightmare before her. Findlay, - no, she could no longer call him by that name. The man she knew no longer existed. He *was* Jack - Jack the Ripper.

Reluctantly, she opened her eye, forcing herself to focus past the monstrosity, to the shelving beyond. The sight was no less horrendous. A woman's head stared back at her though the glass of an over-sized specimen jar.

Viola clutched at her stomach once more. Taylor was still groaning in the next room. His regurgitations made it difficult for her to concentrate on resisting the next wave of nausea.

Henry held his breath and ushered Viola from the fetid crypt. Abberline grimaced and slammed the door behind them.

"Damn lunatic bastard!" he cursed.

Taylor continued to relieve himself of his stomach contents.

"If you are quite done, Taylor, I think we're still in need of an alternate exit." Abberline's voice was shaky.

Taylor wiped his chin as he stood to attention. "Yes, sir."

Henry held Viola tightly; one arm encircled her waist, the other around her shoulders.

"I will excuse your language in front of the lady, Inspector. There are extenuating circumstances," said Henry quietly.

The Inspector raised his eyebrow. "I do apologise."

Viola released herself from Henry's protective embrace. She held her head high and looked the Inspector directly in the eye. She swallowed, fighting another wave of nausea.

"No need, Inspector. I am not a closeted maiden prone to the vapours. I have seen worse horrors in dissection class," she said. "We need to find a way out of this butcher shop before Jack returns." She turned and started searching for an exit, leaving the men to exchange wide-eyed glances.

Henry shook his head and smiled.

"I need to find his work notes," He muttered as he strode off to the desk and started rifling through the drawers.

Viola wandered over to the south wall. The familiar clop of horses' hooves on the cobblestone street, drifted down from the chink in the boarded up window. The carriage stopped. A whip cracked. The clatter of the carriage and hooves faded away.

Viola tapped on the walls with the remnants of a mechanical arm. The dull thuds reminded her of hooves on bare earth, of ordinary, reassuring noises of urban civility. She closed her eye and tilted her head toward the wall, just as she had read in her favourite detective story, and strained to hear any change in the timbre of her knocking.

Taylor watched her for a short time and began his own investigations on the brick wall opposite. Abberline followed him a few steps behind.

Viola tapped her way along the wood-panelled walls until she reached the desk in the far corner, where Henry sat reading though a pile of loose-leafed notes. She glanced down at him. The papers rustled as he shuffled them. He occasionally paused, mumbled and shoved a wad of paper into a large doctor's bag by his chair. Henry glanced up from the pile of papers and grinned.

"There are some most intriguing notes on blood experiments and organ replacement," he said. "Some absolutely incredible theories." His eyes snapped back to the papers. The shuffling intensified.

Viola leaned across the desk and tapped.

Tap. Tap. Tap.

Thunk.

The papers in Henry's hand fell silent. He stared at the wall before them. Viola drew a quick breath and tapped again.

Thunk.

"And you said those detective novels were a waste of time," she said.

Henry shoved the last of the pages into the leather bag and jumped up. The chair crashed to the stone floor. He pulled at the desk. It swung away from the wall, pivoting on one of the rear legs, which remained attached to the floor.

Abberline rushed toward them, waving a collection of mechanical diagrams still clutched in his hand.

"Have you found a way out?" he asked.

Viola dropped the mechanical limb. Her fingers trembled as she ran her hands along the edges of the wall panels. Her hand froze.

Something cold.

Viola bit her lip. She removed one of her gloves and re-positioned her hand near the edge of the panel. A faint tickle of air caressed her finger tip.

"It could be another secret door," she said.

She clawed at the edge of the panel, curling her finger under the rim. Nothing moved.

"Taylor, over here," yelled Abberline. He shoved the blueprints at Henry and joined the search on the adjoining panels.

Viola pressed the panelled surfaces before her.

"There must be a lever, or..." Her voice trailed off. She turned her head toward the smashed Ascension Chamber. "Can you smell that?" she asked.

Abberline sniffed at the air. "Smell what?"

Taylor abandoned his search and returned to the Ascension Chamber. Small wisps of smoke curled out from the crack at the bottom of the jammed door. He placed his palm against the door.

"It is hot, sir!" Taylor frowned, as he recoiled from the door. "Smoke rises, doesn't it, sir?" he asked.

"That must be a bloody big fire," Abberline replied.

Viola resumed her frantic search. The three men joined her in pushing, pummelling and leaning on the wall.

Her heart raced.

Concentrate. Think this out logically.

She took a slow breath. *The latch was on the desk upstairs.*

"The desk," Viola exclaimed. "Why is one leg grounded?"

With one quick movement, Henry swept everything off the top of the desk. His hands skimmed over its surface, then along the edges. He ripped out the drawer and reached into the cavity left behind, scrabbling his fingers along every possible surface. There was a loud click. Henry stood back.

A series of whirs and ratcheting noises crawled along the wall. The panel Viola was leaning on slipped to one side, dragging Viola's hand with it and pulling her off balance. She fell, face forward, into the gaping maw before her and landed with a thud, followed by a flurry of lace and silk as the several layers of skirt settled around her. A faint hissing noise circled around the walls, followed by a clacking noise. The wall behind her slammed shut, cutting off the cellar's artificial light.

Vague shapes slowly formed in the darkness, as Viola's vision adapted to the meagre snippet of light drizzling into the cavity in which she was now trapped. She could hear the faint mumble of Henry's voice calling from the cellar, then silence. A hurried pounding on the wall ensued.

Viola manoeuvred herself to her feet; not an easy task in a full corset. Her hands connected with the walls on either side of her. She was entombed in a cabinet-like room. It was not unlike the Ascension Chamber that had ferried them down into the bowels of Jack's lair. However there was one exception, this chamber would accommodate only two bodies, at most.

Viola turned to examine the source of light near the ceiling. Rough wooden boards were nailed over a window. One was partially loosened. She stretched up on her toes and grabbed at the edge of the loose board. She wrenched it toward her. A loud crack heralded a shower of dirt and wood slivers.

She threw her arms above her head as she toppled backwards into the wall behind her. Her lungs complained again, trying to expel the grimy fragments swirling around her. Sharp pains shot through her palm. She examined her hand. Small beads of blood welled up along deep scratches.

Calm. I must remain calm.

She took a deep breath, catching the faint acrid smell of burning wood.

The wall behind her shuddered, under a renewed onslaught from her companions in the cellar.

Henry!

Viola closed her eye. Her hand throbbed, her back ached.

The smoke was unmistakable now. It flittered down her throat and rushed into her lungs. They writhed for a short time, threatening to deprive Viola of their oxygen.

She gasped for air.

She dragged herself to her feet, snatched up the ruffles of her overskirt and wrapped the train around her hand. It tugged on her bustle, as she reached up toward the boards.

Viola's breaths quickened. She glanced back at the wall behind her. Everything was quiet.

Too quiet.

There was no time to tarry. She reached under her skirt and unhooked the tapes that held the meticulous folds in place. She stood on tip-toes and latched her silk-wrapped hand onto the remnants of the wood, ripping it from the casement.

Fragments fell onto her face. She blinked. The grit scratched her eyeball. Protective tears ran down her cheek.

Don't give up now.

She slowly opened her eye and squinted into the light. The opening was barely a foot high and partly bricked over. A remnant of a barred cellar window was just visible.

What would Holmes do?

Viola closed her eye and wiped the dust from her lashes. *He would assess their resources.*

Above her, more bricks teetered ominously in the window casement.

She shook her purse. The contents rattled: a comb, a policeman's whistle, a small mirror. *I must remember to pack a penny knife next time.* She slipped her purse back under her skirt.

What else do I have?

Viola surveyed the floor of the crypt. Fragments of broken wood and brick lay strewn under a thick layer of dirt and dry, crumbled mortar.

Pain spiked through her palm as she sifted her way through the debris, looking for inspiration. She unwrapped her hand. A splinter of wood was embedded in one of the wounds. She tugged at the offending shard and inspected the laceration. It was deep.

Viola examined the remnants of wood surrounding her. Sharp points projected from the rubble.

If they could cut through skin, perhaps...

Viola glanced up at the crumbling mortar of the brickwork above her. She kicked the debris aside and seized the most savage-looking spear of wood she could find. She braced her back against the wall. Her boot connected with the opposite wall, with a thud. She shifted her heel until she found her balance, and pushed off with her other foot, landing it next to the first. Her bustle slipped. Viola gasped, thrusting her buttocks into the wall to halt her descent. Her stomach plummeted in sympathy. Blood thundered through her ears; her heart pounded.

It seemed so effortless in novels.

Viola squeezed her eye shut and swallowed, tasting the dust that crawled down her nostrils.

I can do this. She sniffed. The smell of smoke was getting stronger. *I must do this.*

Viola crawled her way, slowly testing and repositioning one foot after the other. She pushed her back against the wall, repositioning her feet to keep her balance and leaned over to gouge the loose mortar with her timber shiv. Fragments of brickwork littered the air.

Viola's lungs convulsed. Coughs spasmed throughout her body. The wood fell from her hand and clattered on the floor, followed by a shower of brick, sand and lime. Each breath filled her lungs with more of the powdery concoction. Her head spun; she clutched at the bars to steady herself.

Missed.

She fell, landing with a thwack and a scream. The pain returned, searing through her wrist and into her forearm. Viola winced. Several unyielding masses pressed into her torso. Jagged bricks poked into her arm, others compressed her ankle. She scrabbled to extract herself from the ever-growing pile of rubble.

Bricks scraped and shifted, drowned out by a protracted ripping sound. Viola inspected her once-pristine skirts. The ruffle had been torn from the hem in several places. Bows hung limply from the soiled silk. Small ribbon rosettes littered the debris surrounding her.

Tendrils of smoke crept through the crack under the door. They twisted around Viola's arm and slithered up her neck.

She cupped her hands against the panel.

"Henry, Inspector Abberline," she yelled and pounded on the wall, "can you hear me?" *Please be alive.*

She pressed her ear to the wood. There was a muffled... something. A faint pounding on the wall, from the other side? She frowned.

"Find the latch to open the door," she yelled.

There was no reply.

Viola kicked the wall. Throbbing pangs grabbed at her ankle and shot up into her leg. She placed her foot on the ground. The tendon ached but her foot held its own. She clenched her fists and pounded the wall.

I am not helpless.

Shadows flittered across the walls of her wooden crypt. Viola turned to the window. Her eye widened.

Someone is out there!

Abberline had ordered Smith to search the rooms above. He knew they were in the cellar. Surely he would have seen the fire and be looking for another access to the cellar. Viola prayed he would hear her cries.

She stood on tiptoe and yelled. There was no reply.

A set of black shiny shoes raced silently past the window. *No sound at all.*

She pulled a coin from her purse and threw it at the window. It tinged off the surface and fell to the floor.

Glass! Clever. The crypt, just like the cellar, had been built to stifle any noises that emanated from the laboratory.

Viola bit her lip. She hefted her bag in her hand and smiled. She unwound the long cord straps and swung the bag at the window, resulting in a satisfactory smash and much dodging of glass shards.

Viola's ankle twinged as it rolled on a loose brick.

I can't climb the walls again.

She snatched up her skirts, ripped off a section of spoilt ruffle, wrapped it around her hand and set to stacking the fallen bricks to form a step ladder, of sorts. She clamoured up the mound and pulled herself closer, her chin almost level to the bottom of the window.

She caught her breath. The gutter smell of excrement and rubbish was strangely welcoming after the smoke and decaying odours of the cellar's secrets.

Someone yelled in the distance. Wheels clattered at high speed over the cobblestones. Footsteps followed.

A wave of relief swept over Viola. She placed a hand on the wall to steady herself.

"Down here!" she yelled.

Silence.

"Please, can anyone hear me?"

There was a shuffle of feet. A pair of well-worn shoes and grey trousers filled the window frame. A silver-tipped cane clicked on the cobblestones beside them.

"Hello?" said Viola.

The shoes turned to face the window.

"Hello." The voice was familiar.

Viola shivered. The blood ran from her cheeks. Her hands trembled as she wrenched the compact mirror from her bag. A faint crack ran through its surface, where it had hit one of the bars in the window.

Viola tilted the mirror until she could see her would-be-rescuer. He wore a large black coat. A glint of brass flashed under one sleeve. The man crouched down, laid his cane on the ground and peeked through the broken window.

"Fancy meeting you here, my dear Viola."

Viola's stomach dropped. The mirror fell into a mound of brick. She swallowed the wave of nausea that surged up her throat.

"Please help me..." Her voice quivered faintly. "... James."

"The name is Jack, but I am sure you know that by now."

Jack held his billy-cock hat in his hand. He flicked her red feather that was sewn securely in the hatband, another feather wedged beside it.

Two feathers?

Viola struggled to slow her breathing. Her pulse continued to throb in her ears.

"Seems like you are in a bit of a pickle," said Jack.

"It seems that way," replied Viola. *Breathe.*

"It is a shame the Fire Brigade will most likely arrive too late." Jack leaned down and whispered through the bars. "It's not safe in Whitechapel, you know."

Viola measured her breaths, slowing each one in turn.

"Please, you cannot leave us here," she said.

"Why not?" He sniffed the feather.

Viola's muscles cringed. She forced a weak smile.

"Because you were once our friend." Her stomach churned as she said the words. *There has to be some spark of humanity left, not consumed by Jack the Ripper.*

"Was I?" Jack scoffed. "You are collecting quite a merry band of sweethearts aren't you, Viola. Donell, now Henry." He paused, turning his hat over in his hands. "Perhaps I just wanted to meet your sister Anne? She was such an adorable creature." He chuckled. "So much more... accommodating."

What did you do to Anne!

"Please, James," said Viola. "Tell me what you did..." She cleared her throat. "Tell me what happened to Anne."

"Why should I? James was a fool. I am not," said Jack. "Your family has brought me nothing but pain, Viola. Anne was the only one of you who cared." He slapped his hat against his leg. "And even she betrayed me in the end."

Viola bit her tongue. Her face wrinkled in pain as she tried to hold back the tears and not cry out.

"Please," she said. "I just need to know what happened to Anne. I'll do anything."

"Anything?" Jack asked. He sniffed at the air. His voice was calm, measured. "The fire is progressing nicely. I shall have to leave you soon."

Viola could smell it too. She glanced through the window. Clouds of grey smoke unfurled along the alley outside.

Time was running out.

"If I told you what I did to your sister, would you do anything I demand?" ask Jack.

Viola's heart fluttered, preparing to implode. *Is Anne still alive? I need to know.* She nodded slowly.

"If I told you what I did to Anne, would you come with me? Would you come with me, stay with me, and not betray me, Viola?" He narrowed his eyes. "Would you leave Henry Collins to perish in the flames?"

Viola's heart clenched; for a moment it forgot how to beat. It dropped in her chest.

"That would be murder," she replied.

"Ah, but you would know what happened to your sister, after all these years." Jack grinned. "Surely the truth is worth a little sacrifice."

Viola closed her eye. She imagined Henry gasping for air, suffocating in the smoke, the flames licking at his treasured waistcoat, the spark fading from his brilliant blue eyes. She grabbed at her chest.

Not my Henry. She could not leave him. A tear escaped and rolled down one cheek. *Not even for Anne.*

Viola peered out the window. Jack's cane lay near the window grille. The silver dog head stared coldly back at her. Mocking her.

"The needs of the many outweigh the needs of the one," she said.

Jack laughed. "A noble sentiment. So much for family loyalty. Your father *will* be disappointed you could not recover his beloved Anne." He leaned in closer to the window. "I do hope dear Henry appreciates your sacrifice, Viola."

Jack smirked. He stared into Viola's eye. His pupils widened. Viola grit her teeth and stared back. She held her breath.

I will not flinch. I will not let you win.

The smell of smoke grew stronger.

Viola did not blink.

A fire bell clanged in the distance.

She held her gaze.

Her eyes stung, moisture welling in the corner of her eye.

She raised her eyebrow, opening her eye and fought the urge to blink.

A carriage rattled along the nearby street. The fire bell grew louder.

Jack's eyelids fluttered. The smirk fell from his face. He glanced over his shoulder. The bell clanged along the street and past the end of the alley. The shouting remained at a distance. He leaned in closer.

Viola lifted her head and straightened her shoulders. *I win.*

"Tell me what happened to Anne," she said calmly.

"I did nothing to her," he whispered. "I'm not responsible for her disappearance." He glanced at the feathers in his hat band. "I want you to know. You made me what I am. You and your sister Anne," he hissed.

"No, that can't be true," insisted Viola.

"It is the truth," replied Jack. "I swear on my mother's grave." He glanced toward the cellar beyond. "And soon to be yours as well."

"That thing in there was...?" Viola swallowed. If she spoke the words, there was no turning back.

"Ah, so you have finally met mother?" said Jack.

The full horror formed in her consciousness, flooding her memory and erasing any early memories of her once-friend. James was dead. The monster, who called himself Jack the Ripper, was fully gestated.

Viola gagged. She opened her mouth. No words came.

"Mother was always supportive of my work, and still is. The answer was in the blood, you see. My theory is valid," Jack explained.

Viola's heart raced. She leaned back into the deep shadows. Fingers of smoke felt their way along the floor. They reached up, clutching at her skirt. Viola swatted her hand at the grey mist, scattering it along the floor. The muted thuds on the wall to the cellar were becoming less frequent. She fancied she heard coughing.

Perhaps they're still alive? I can't let them die. I can't let Henry die. She had to convince Jack to free them from his laboratory - the cellar.

The cellar!

"You can't let the cellar burn," said Viola. "Your work will be destroyed."

Jack chuckled.

"That's the intention," he said. "Soon the flames reach my little surprise." Jack grabbed the bars of the window and pressed his face up against them. Glass crunched under his feet. "There is a cache of explosives, designed to obliterate any evidence and any curious interlopers."

Viola floundered in her reticule for a pen and paper.

I need to warn them.

She scribbled a note and fed it under the closed door, into the cellar. It was snatched from her grasp.

Someone is still alive.

"No matter. My research is almost complete. They will provide me with a new lab. I am very useful to them."

"Who will provide for you?" Viola asked.

"You have seen them. They are everywhere, The Men in Grey."

Viola searched her memories. Commercial Street station, the Magic Lantern Show, poor little Elly... *My dirigible with the pink ribbons.* The men in grey suits were not a *figment of her over-read imagination,* as the Inspector had decreed. Viola smiled.

I knew it!

"Who are the Men in Grey?" asked Viola.

"Always the detective, even in the face of death," replied Jack.

"Then what harm can it do to tell me?" she asked.

"You know how to play the game," Jack replied. He clicked his tongue. "Very well. I will give you this: They call themselves The Society. They are ghosts in the Great Machine, trying to free the rusty cogs from the Imperial constraints, decided by a Queen who has outlived her time. They cast their shadows all over the Empire. They infiltrate unseen."

"Are they Anarchists?" asked Viola.

"They are powerful. And they look after their own. They recruited me at University. They saw my ..." Jack toyed with the red feather once more. "...my potential. They provided me with everything I need to pursue my research and gave me a purpose."

A small explosion rocked the crypt. It echoed along the street above. Jack jumped to his feet. Viola scrabbled on the floor next to her, for the pocket mirror. She struggled to her feet, angling the mirror to spy Jack through the window. He looked worried.

Jack squatted back down, toad-like in both demeanour and posture.

"I can but have one last joy," he grinned. He licked his lips. "Hearing your friends suffer."

"No!" Viola screamed. "Someone will find us."

"There is no one else to help you," said Jack.

"Constable Smith will find another way in," replied Viola.

She wrapped her fingers around the head of the cane and yanked it through the bars. She twirled it in her hand and thrust the heavy dog-head towards Jack's face.

Jack rocked back on his haunches. A crooked smile flickered over his lips.

"He is one of ours, dear girl."

"No, you're lying," she said.

Jack straightened his back and took a deep breath.

"You don't trust me? Oh Viola, I am mortally wounded." One corner of Jack's mouth curled upward. "But just to show you I have no hard feelings, I will let you know a secret. Every fox hole has a back door." He grinned. "You like to play detective. It shouldn't be too hard to puzzle it out. But you'd better hurry. *Tempus fugit.*"

Viola's mind raced. She struggled to catch her breath as her heart knocked at her ribcage, trying to free itself of its prison.

A secret door? She scanned the walls. *They are just plain walls.*

Tempus fugit.

Another bell clanged. Much closer this time. Men shouted.

Jack released his grip on the window bars.

"It was nice meeting you again, Viola." He kissed her red feather on his hat band. "It has been entertaining. Adieu, my sweet. I shall remember you always."

"You can't leave us here," yelled Viola.

The grey trousers and well-worn shoes turned and sauntered away. There was gunfire, running footsteps.

"Somebody help," screamed Viola. The commotion continued. Viola pounded the crypt's walls with the walking cane, and wept.

Tempus fugit.

Viola crumpled to the floor. There was no way out of the crypt.

Jack lied.

She lifted her face to the heavens. Fine spider webs clung to the ceiling, swept away where she had climbed up earlier. Broken strands fluttered in the breeze from the alley. They licked the edge of a small brass tube in one corner of the ceiling.

Strange place for a pipe.

Viola leaned on the walking cane, pulled herself to her feet and stood directly under the pipe. It was little over an inch in diameter.

Not enough light to see inside.

She flicked the cane upward and tapped the pipe. The sound rang through the crypt, ringing in her eardrums.

Viola drove the tip of the cane into the pipe. A loud click vibrated down the shaft. A low grinding echoed through the crypt. Viola spun around, searching for the source of the noise.

A panel in a side wall inched upward, stopping half way. It quivered. The grinding halted, replaced by a high-pitched scream. Viola poked her head through the low hatchway. A network of pipes ran up one side of the opening. Chains ran up from the door and along the roof to a series of pulleys. Gears and rods gyrated, shaking faster as fine jets of steam screamed though tiny cracks in the pipes.

Viola dashed back into the crypt and pounded on the wall to the cellar.

"I've found a way out," she yelled.

She pressed her ear against the wall. She could hear nothing but the street noises filtering down through the window behind her.

Don't you dare be dead, Henry Collins. Wait for me.

She hitched up the hem of her tattered skirts, tucked it into her waistband and crawled through the hatchway and emerged into a cramped, excavated grotto. A puff of dust followed her, glittering in the faint shaft of light that spilt in from the crypt. Perspiration beaded on her forehead and clung to her skin.

She ran her fingers along the walls. Dirt crumbled to the floor. Her hand knocked against a rough wooden beam. It shivered under the assault. A lantern knocked against the wood. Viola lit the wick. Its warm glow reflected off wet patches along the walls. A narrow tunnel had been dug at the back of the grotto. Several more beams braced the walls at uncomfortably irregular intervals.

The tunnel turned toward the street above, ending in a web-infested ladder wedged hard up against a partially bricked wall. Viola wielded the cane, cutting through the webs and tearing them from the ladder.

She lowered her boot onto the lower rung and tested it with her weight.

Seems solid.

She ran her hands along the rails. The humidity had already started to soften the wood in some places.

Viola scrabbled up the ladder. A cylindrical shaft continued a few feet further. She stepped on the top rung and stretched up into the shaft, squeezing her bustle into the tube. A heavy iron cover sealed the exit above.

Another explosion rumbled along the tunnel, from the cellar. *Too close.* The walls around her vibrated in unison with their timber supports. Clumps of soil showered down from the roof and spat off walls. Beam joints squeaked. Pipework in the grotto shuddered. Gears rattled.

Viola clung to the sides of the shaft, as the ladder jolted under her feet.

Horus est; the hour is up.

Viola pounded on the metal plate, as she bellowed. "Down here!"

Aftershocks rumbled through the ground around her, reverberating in the metal cover above her.

Viola screamed one last time. The footsteps slowed as they neared the lid above her. There was a thud on the metal plate.

"I thought I heard something." The muffled voice was close.

Viola hefted up the cane and bashed its dog-head on the bottom of the plate.

"Down here," she yelled.

The plate wiggled. There was a faint scraping. Flecks of metal dripped onto Viola's shoulders. The plate jerked and rotated, excruciatingly slowly. A long, hollow grinding echoed down the shaft and resonated in her ear drums.

Pale hands emerged at the edge of the plate and hefted it free. The shaft inhaled the roar of flames and choking smoke muffling the clatter of the plate on the cobblestones.

A fresh-faced constable peered into the opening. Smudges of soot were smeared across his chin and forehead. He ran his gaze over her clothing and frowned.

"Are you all right, Miss?" he asked.

"I've had better days," she replied.

"How did you get down there, Miss?"

"Through the main building. There's an Ascension Box in the main building. Doctor Collins, Inspector Abberline and his men are trapped in the cellar," replied Viola. "You must hurry."

The Constable's eyes widened.

"The Inspector is in the cellar?" He shook his head. "The entire building is on fire. We can't get in that way."

"You'll have to come this way then. There's a tunnel. It leads to the cellar but you'll have to break through," instructed Viola. "Please hurry. The building is rigged with explosives."

"Explosives!" The Constable turned and yelled for help. "Righty oh, Miss. Out you come. It's not safe here." He offered her his hand.

Viola shook her head and backed down the ladder.

"I'm not going anywhere until they are free," she said.

Viola led two Constables along the tunnel to the crypt. One carried a pick axe, the other hefted a sledgehammer. They carried their tools low, studying the walls and avoiding the support beams as they jogged after her.

Viola ducked through the hatchway and started pounding on the closed door to the cellar. She examined the bottom of the door. Thick smoke drifted around her boots. It clawed at her stockings and the tattered remnants of her hem. It had been some time since she had heard noises from the cellar.

Please be alive.

"Please stand back in the tunnel, Miss," said the fresh-faced Constable.

Viola retreated to the hatchway. She eyed the hissing pipes that surrounded the exit and wondered if they would survive another explosion.

There was a loud crack from the crypt. A thunk shook the wall beside her. Gears screeched and tumbled above the ceiling. Viola darted back into the crypt. The constables backed away from the wall and gaped at the ceiling. With a shudder, the door jolted an inch and stopped.

"No," Viola screamed. She grabbed the edge of the door and pulled. *I am not leaving without you!*

The constables dropped their tools and joined her. A sudden jolt knocked Viola back into the crypt. The door slid open.

A wall of heat rolled over Viola. Thick grey smoke filled the crypt, obscuring her vision. She shoved her makeshift silk bandage over her nose. She could hear coughing in the smog-filled cellar.

"Henry!" she yelled. "Over here."

The coughing grew louder. Three figures emerged from the smoke and stumbled into the crypt. They wore dark, shaped-leather masks, with large dark lenses, surrounded by brass cylinders, for eyes. A short, ribbed hose emerged from the snout into two large cylinders. The fresh-faced Constable reeled from the sight. The other Constable raised his sledgehammer and stepped between them and Viola.

Henry peeled off the mask and coughed.

"It is all right, Constable," said Viola, as she pushed past him and dragged Henry to the hatchway.

Viola poked her head back through the hole in the alley cobblestones. Henry wiggled up the shaft. He winced as the rough edges snagged

threads of his favourite waistcoat. He reached up and dragged himself through the exit hole. The waistcoat's third button pulled on the edge of the manhole.

Henry stopped and glanced at Viola. She bit her lip, trying not to smirk.

"Polly's cake?" she whispered.

Henry frowned. Viola grabbed his hand and pulled. The silver button popped from the material and plopped into the tunnel. Henry crawled onto the ground and slammed his mask on the stones.

"Damn," he said.

Viola leaned into the shaft.

"Hurry up, Inspector," she said. "The building could explode at any minute."

Inspector Abberline removed his mask and leaned against a wooden beam, gasping for breath. He surveyed the shaft and eyed the exit hole. His eyes widened.

He glanced at his waist, grimaced and clenched his teeth.

"Bollocks!" he grumbled.

He climbed half way up the ladder and threw the doctor's bag up through the hole.

"Tell those Constables to hurry up," he said.

Jack pulled up the collar of his thick wool coat then tugged down the sleeves, ensuring his wrists were covered. He tapped his new bowler so that it sat low on his brow, and ran his finger along the silver thread of the red feather that was tucked neatly in its band.

The sky was clear, allowing the fog to seep between the dockyard buildings. He slipped easily through the gloom, unseen by prying eyes as he hurried to his rendezvous. He chuckled as he jumped a large puddle, landing on the edge of the footpath.

Trolley wheels clattered and bounced on the cobble stones behind him, as his valet grumbled and struggled to keep up. The luggage-laden trolley jolted to an abrupt halt as it hit the gutter. The valet groaned. He leaned into the trolley and edged it up onto the footpath, then kicked one of the wheels back into alignment.

Jack's grin widened.

"Keep up!"

Jack heard muffled voices as they neared the dock. He slowed his pace, motioning for the valet to halt.

"Stay here," he demanded, "and not a word."

Jack edged closer, cocking his ear towards the conversation. The voices were faint, hidden somewhere ahead in the maze of old buildings and fog. He moved onward towards them.

"There's always a problem when a wild dog gets the taste for blood. It either has to be sent away or be put down." Jack recognised the voice of Mr Browne.

"What fate has The Society pronounced for him?" asked his co-conspirator.

"We have invested much in him, Mr Grey." There was a pause, then Mr Browne continued. "But it will depend on his next step."

Mr Grey scoffed. "Do you think they can control him?"

"The Society can control everyone. Eventually," said Mr Browne.

"And when we have them, they are ours for life." Mr Grey chuckled.

"As long as they are of use," replied Mr Browne.

Mr Grey cleared his throat.

Jack stepped into the cramped courtyard. Talons of fog clawed at his woollen coat, unwilling to abandon him. His footsteps rang loudly on the cobblestones.

"Good evening, Jack," said Mr Browne. "Excellent timing, as usual."

Jack nodded.

"Glad you could join us," Mr Browne swept his arm in the direction of his associate. "You have met Mr Grey?"

"Ah yes. Mr Grey was kind enough to supply an alibi for my time in Marylebone," said Jack, extending his left hand in greeting.

Mr Browne took an expeditious step away from Mr Grey.

The ring of metal echoed loudly in the murky courtyard, as Jack's blade slid from its holster to greet Mr Grey. He groaned and grabbed his stomach. His eyes widened. A furrow deepened on his forehead as his eyebrows wrinkled. Water welled in his eyes. He turned to Mr Browne. His knees betrayed him.

"Why?" he gasped.

"Because you belong to us and, now you are known to The Metropolitan Police Force, you have become a liability. Abberline has been looking for you."

Mr Browne plucked his fob watch from his waistcoat pocket and flicked it open.

"The ship will be sailing soon, Jack. Best not miss it." He snapped the cover shut and turned his back on Mr Grey.

Jack stooped down and, with a quick flick, ended Mr Grey's pain.

He picked up Mr Grey's bowler, dusted it off and handed it to Mr Browne.

"You can smell the sea from here," said Mr Browne. He took a deep breath then slowly exhaled.

"And dog shit," said Jack, as he handed Mr Grey's hat to Mr Browne. "And where is your new lapdog?"

"Awaiting my command," replied Mr Browne.

Viola glanced at the new book Henry had given her, *The Great Bank Robbery*. Its green cover peeked out from remnants of brown paper. He had presented her with a new novel every week since their encounter in the cellar. Four in all. She didn't have the heart to tell him she had already read it.

Henry grinned as he poured a second teaspoon of sugar into his tea. Viola offered him a piece of Polly's fruitcake. He licked his lips, declined and poured another cup of black tea.

The cup rattled onto the saucer as he stifled another cough. They were indeed fortunate to be alive, having only just escaped from the smoke-filled tunnel before the entire building had been consumed in flames.

True to Jack's word, nothing of his laboratory had survived. The cellar, along with its precious evidence, had been reduced to ashes. The preliminary notes on his ocular transplant experiments had remained forgotten on the cellar floor, where Viola had dropped them, and incinerated in the ensuing fireball.

All had been lost, save a few handfuls of blueprints and research notes, which Inspector Abberline had seized off the benches, stuffed into a doctor's bag and tossed up the manhole into the alley. *Quick thinking on his part.*

After a week of worry, the Whitechapel Police surgeon had finally declared all three of her companions fit. Henry and Constable Taylor had been only a few days in his care.

If only Jack knew the irony of it. His Chemical Filtration Masks had saved their lives.

Abberline had not fared as well however, having been forced to linger in the smoke-filled tunnel. With the help of Sir Archibald and his mechanical lung, Abberline had been restored to almost full health; though this had not stopped his incessant complaints on the lack of cigar-smoking in his foreseeable future.

Viola took a deep breath, puffed her cheeks and expelled the captured breath in a deep sigh. Normality had been restored. Life in Marylebone had been quiet. *Too quiet.* No adventures, no mysteries, even no newspaper reporters. Abberline had made good his promise in keeping their names out of the paper.

"Why doesn't the Inspector contact us?" said Viola.

"There is obviously nothing to report," Henry replied.

"Surely they must have found him by now?"

"Admit it, Viola. There have been no more Ripper murders. Findlay is gone." Henry glanced at the fruitcake.

"But..."

"Viola," he said, "you have no need to worry about him anymore. His superiors would not risk him remaining to draw attention to The Society. The Men in Grey will have made certain to cover their tracks."

"What if..."

"You can't spend the rest of your life thinking 'what if'." Henry placed a warm hand on Viola's and looked directly into her eye. "He won't bother you anymore. Let him go. I do not want to have to compete with *another* ghost for the rest of my life."

Viola's eye widened. Her cheeks flushed.

"What are you saying, Henry?"

A loud tapping on the parlour door snatched Henry's attention away from Viola. Polly entered, her gaze falling toward their entwined hands. She cleared her throat.

"Inspector Abberline is here to see you, Miss. He says it's important."

Henry released Viola's hand, deftly retrieved a piece of fruitcake from the tray and leaned back into his chair.

"Thank you, Polly. Show him in. Oh, and bring a fresh pot of tea, please."

Polly nodded.

"And will you be wanting something else, Doctor Collins?"

Henry swallowed, wiped a few crumbs from his moustache and

shook his head.

Viola rolled her eye. Polly smiled as she left.

A rich, earthy scent followed Inspector Abberline as he entered the room. He coughed as he sat down.

"Good afternoon." His voice rasped as he struggled to catch his breath.

"Inspector, have you been smoking your cigars?" asked Henry.

"And what if I have, Doctor Collins?" he grumbled.

"Against doctor's orders?" asked Viola.

"Are you going to tell on me?" the Inspector asked.

Viola glanced at the Inspector as she offered him a piece of fruitcake.

"I will make you a deal, Doctor Stewart." The Inspector placed an oversized leather satchel on his lap. "If you do not tell him, I will share something with you, about Doctor Findlay and his employers."

A frown flashed over Viola's brow. She swallowed, trying to return the moisture to her throat.

"Firstly, I have read through the papers we collected and found some interesting information." He laid some papers out on the table between them. "There appears to be a clandestine anarchist group not only funding Findlay's research, but also orchestrating his nefarious activities as well. Fortunately for us, you seem to have stumbled upon their plot against the Queen herself, Doctor Stewart. Unfortunately, they've been extremely careful in their communications. But there was a name, of sorts."

The Inspector produced his notebook and flipped through the pages.

"A '*Mr B*'. There really wasn't much definite information, but there was this symbol."

Viola's frown deepened. *He was telling the truth.*

Henry raised his eyebrow and leaned forward in his chair.

The Inspector handed over his notebook. In the middle of the page, hand-drawn in pencil, was a symbol: a cog with an ouroboros laid upon it, not quite devouring its tail, and the centre spokes shaped in an 'S'.

"Jack said they call themselves The Society," said Viola.

"I spoke to the Yard," said Abberline. "They weren't aware this organisation existed, let alone had such lofty ambitions." He paused to cough into his large handkerchief. "There have been reported sightings of similarly dressed men at various riots in the area. But then again, grey is a favoured colour this year. Even my missus has a fancy for it." Abberline ran his hand over his eyes, and massaged his temple.

Viola smiled. "Then you agree I am not living in a fantasy world, Inspector?"

Inspector Abberline grimaced.

"I apologise for doubting you, Doctor Stewart," he said.

"Apology accepted, Inspector," replied Viola.

Henry offered Abberline a cup of tea.

"Did Constable Smith provide any enlightenment?" Henry asked.

"Not so far. This Society is smart," replied Abberline. "It seems any real information is restricted to only those who need to know. We need to find this 'Mr B'. It seems he is the local contact." He stifled a dry cough.

Viola bit her lip.

"What about that Mr Grey," asked Viola.

"Ah yes, Mr Grey. He hasn't been found yet. But, that brings me to my second bit of information. I thought you should know before the papers publish it." Abberline rubbed his sideburns and retrieved a large envelope-like folder from his bag. "We have been more fortuitous in finding Mr Findlay."

Viola heart skipped.

"You have found him?" asked Henry.

"In a matter of speaking," replied the Inspector. He handed the folder to Viola. "I would not usually show such items to a lady but, as you have said yourself, Doctor Stewart, you have seen worse things in dissection class."

Viola took a deep breath and nodded. *You were listening.* She slid the photographs from the folder.

"Where did you find him?" she asked.

"In the Thames, on New Year's Eve," Abberline replied. "It appears the body had been there for some time."

Henry examined the photographs.

"But how did you identify the body, with such extensive damage to the face?" he asked.

Abberline reached into the folder, pulled out another photo and handed it to Viola.

"This hat was found with the body. It is Findlay's hat, is it not?"

Henry nodded.

Viola stared at the photograph: a plain grey billy-cock hat with traces of mud under the brim and *one* plain feather. The feather that had been twin to hers when last seen. Viola shook her head slowly.

This feather had only been wedged into the band and remained intact. Her feather had been sewn into the band, yet it was now missing. Unlikely. If Jack was alive, he would not have parted with his trophy.

Viola placed the photograph on the table and closed her eyes. She covered her mouth. She could feel her warm breath on her hand, fast and shallow. *Breathe.* Viola measured her breaths, each one for an extra count.

"It's not Findlay's body," she whispered.

The two men looked at each other.

"A grey billy-cock with a red feather. I'm sure it's his hat," said Henry.

"It is his hat but..." She turned the photograph to face Henry and tapped on the feather. "There is only one feather."

"Yes," replied Henry.

"When I saw him in the alley, he had two feathers in his hat," she replied.

"The other one must have fallen out," said Abberline. "The body was in the river for over a week."

"The original feather had silver thread twisted around the base and it was sewn into the band. Look here, the stitches were carefully removed. It wasn't torn or ripped."

Abberline pulled out a pair of wire spectacles and perched them on his nose. He examined the photographs closely, squinting as he did so.

"I don't follow," he said.

"It's not just any feather, Inspector. It belonged to me." Viola wrinkled her nose and avoided Abberline's gaze. "The shaft was wound with silver thread. If he was dead, it would still be in the hat. If this is some other poor soul, meant to deceive us, he would never leave it behind."

Henry's hand gently touched Viola's forearm. Viola closed her eye briefly and took a deep breath.

"A hat does not provide a solid identification, Inspector," he offered. "I trust Doctor Stewart's judgement in this."

"The body was also wearing Findlay's clothes and his card was in the coat pocket." Abberline smiled.

"And his mechanical limb?" asked Viola.

"How would a Whitechapel doctor afford a mechanical, or get a permit for that matter?" asked Abberline.

"He had a mechanical?" asked Henry. He studied the photograph of the corpse and passed it to Abberline. "Both of the limbs on the body are intact, Inspector."

"Are you certain?" asked Abberline. "We have no record of any such procedure."

The Inspector flipped to the middle of his notebook, skimmed a few lines, then proceeded to scribble furiously.

Viola nodded.

"I have seen it. James Findlay, Jack, had a mechanical arm. Do you remember the discarded mechanical limbs in the cellar? Who do you think they belonged to?”

“Bollocks,” Abberline cursed quietly. He cleared his throat and continued. “These Men in Grey are cunning blighters.”

“Then we shall have to be more cunning, Inspector,” Viola replied.

“We can’t let the papers get hold of this. We’ve only just got the riots under control,” said Abberline. “I will have to ask you not to share this information.”

The doctors nodded.

Abberline cleared his throat.

“That just leaves one thing,” he said. “There were some letters found amongst Findlay’s papers. They were signed by a Miss Anne Carrington.”

Viola gasped. Her heart plunged into her chest.

“One mentioned you by name,” continued Abberline. “Do you know her?”

“Anne was my sister,” replied Viola.

Henry placed his hand on her shoulder.

Abberline placed a thin bundle of letters, wrapped in a black ribbon, onto the table.

“Have you read them, Inspector?” asked Viola.

Abberline nodded.

“I am sorry, Doctor Stewart. They may have contained evidence related to our investigation.”

Viola picked up the bundle. Her fingers trembled as she pulled the ribbon and unfolded one of the letters. The ink was faint. She held the paper up toward the window. It was definitely Anne’s handwriting.

Dear James,

I do not take up my pen in order to extract a letter from you, but to ask for your understanding. This will be my last opportunity of writing before I leave Edinburgh.

Though honour binds you to me, I cannot in all good conscience hold you to your promise, having discovered you still have ardent thoughts of my sister, Viola.

I scorn to act in any manner that may bring reproach on my family by holding you to our previous clandestine agreement. I am not prepared to give you a life of misery, marrying against your own conscience. I will not be deceived as you deceive yourself.

I now take my leave of Edinburgh and my family's favour, to make my own way in the world and to avoid any scandal.

Anne Carrington.

A faint shadow surrounded Anne's signature. It was a notched circle. Much like a cog. Viola tilted the paper to catch the light behind it. Thin lines traced over the cog: a snake swallowing its tail.

THE END

Acknowledgements

Thank you to my friends, David, Lynne, Sharon, Carole, Terry, James and Zena, for their generosity and dedication.
And thank you to Susan who lit the fire and insisted I write more stories.

About the Author

Karen J Carlisle lives in Adelaide with her family and the ghost of her ancient Devon Rex cat. She loves fantasy fiction, gardening, historical re-creation, and steampunk and can often be found plotting fantastical, piratic or airship adventures.
Karen has always loved chocolate and rarely refuses a cup of tea. She is not keen on South Australian summers.

www.karenjcarlisle.com
https://www.patreon.com/KarenJCarlisle
https://ko-fi.com/karenjcarlisle

Follow me at:
www.goodreads.com/KarenJCarlisle
https://www.instagram.com/karenjcarlisle/
https://www.tiktok.com/@karenjcarlisle
https://twitter.com/kjcarlisle

Other works by Karen J Carlisle

The Adventures of Viola Stewart series:
Available in paperback:
Doctor Jack & Other Tales: Journal #1
Eye of the Beholder & Other Tales: Journal #2
The Illusioneer & Other Tales: Journal #3
Also available as eBooks

Other books by Karen J Carlisle:
The Aunt Enid Mysteries
Aunt Enid: Protector Extraordinaire
A Fey Tale

The Department of Curiosities
The Department of Curiosities
Coming soon:
Against the Empire

Also available as eBooks:
Short Story Collections
With a Twist of the Nib: For when time is short
Another Twist of the Nib: Shorter Tales with a Darker Twist
Quarantine Reads: Escape to Adventure

Mrs Hudson Investigates
Mrs Hudson Investigates
The Case of the Forgotten Letter

from
Eye of the Beholder & Other Tales:
The Adventures of Viola Stewart Journal #2

Mummies.
Murder.
Madness.
in

Eye of the Beholder

Chapter 1:
Something Wicked This Way Comes

The grinding of the heavy double gate set Professor Fosse's teeth on edge. The iron bars rattled as it slammed shut, encasing them in gloom. Gone were the light-filled corridors and airy rooms laid out for public view. Gone were the tranquil chirps of the caged birds kept to pacify the more fortunate inmates. Far-off cries and screechings echoed through the empty hallway before them.

Keys chinked at the Warden's hip. They descended into the bowels of Bedlam, leaving the sane world behind them. The stench of sweat and urine burned his nostrils as he followed the Warden past iron-bound doors. Hinges rattled.

The Warden paused. The way ahead was barred and locked.

Finger gears whirred inside Fosse's left glove. He pulled the leather tighter. His flesh hand trembled. He had not set foot in Bedlam since. . . His heart thumped. *How long had it been?* He took a slow breath, filling his lungs with the foul air. *Not long enough.*

Now he faced the core of pandemonium again. He clenched his lean fingers and straightened his shoulders. It was louder than he remembered.

"Are you certain?" asked the Warden, as the key touched the lock.

Fosse closed his eyes and relaxed his fingers. He was a man of science, of facts. He sucked in the foul air then opened his eyes and nodded.

The Warden lit his lantern. The light sputtered. The rancid smell of tallow filled the corridor.

Beyond the portal lay rows of barred cells, each with its own cacophony of stenches. Fosse breathed through his mouth and stared at the back of the Warden's head. It bobbed along the corridor then turned and jerked toward one of the cells.

"That's him."

A wheezing lump of rags pressed into one corner.

Fosse studied the lump. The Lord Banbury he knew would roar objections, demand his release. This creature cowered in the shadows. *How could I have been so naive? No one remains untouched by twelve months in Bedlam.*

He swallowed. "Are you certain?"

"Dunno what he was once. Only what he is now," said the Warden.

"I need to speak with him. In private."

"He won't talk. Thinks he is being followed. We're all out to get him. Pretty much standard for here." The Warden knocked at the bars with his nightstick.

Banbury's eyes flickered in their direction.

Fosse leaned closer. "Lord Banbury?" He cleared his throat. "Hello. Remember me? Fosse? I need to ask you something. Something important."

Banbury's eyes widened - red and jaundiced. He scuttled to the bars. The gaunt face wedged between the metal. Lice crawled in the beard, somersaulting as the lips mumbled. Stale breath engulfed them. Fosse screwed up his nose and leaned away.

Memories of Bay Rum cologne, of sweat and rancid oil distracted him - pungent, overpowering, always heralding Banbury's return from a dig. Fosse loathed that smell. A wave of nausea washed over him. He now longed for the sickly aroma. *Anything to drown out the stench.*

"What did he say?" he asked.

"He's always rambling on about something. Shadows, curses. Or cats. Pfft."

Banbury lunged at the Warden, spitting out an unintelligible slur of words.

"Yes, yes. We know," grumbled the Warden.

"What was that? What did he say?"

The Warden rolled his eyes. "Beware the eye."

"Beware the eye?"

"He's got a thing about eyes. Careful now. Don't get too close, or he'll try to scratch out yours."

Fosse frowned. Lord Banbury was once a well-respected man of science. Egyptologist. Mentor. This poor creature wasn't the real man; the man who sponsored him. The man who mentored him. The man who forfeited his position at the Museum, the position he now held.

What could've sent you mad?

Fosse dropped four crowns into the Warden's hand. "See he gets new clothes. And a haircut." Another coin fell into the palm. "Good man."

The aroma of spices filled the air. Dark velvet curtains cloaked the windows. Flickering candlelight illuminated rows of occupied, mismatched wooden chairs. Shadows licked the steps of the, as yet unlit, temporary dais and the curtain which concealed the promised spectacle.

Pools of light erupted as a dark-suited young man lit the candelabra around the hall.

Chairs squeaked on the polished floor. The crowd squirmed, stared into the blackness and murmured.

Viola prodded the padding of her chair - a dining chair apparently roped into service to make up numbers.

A candelabra rattled against the dais. Light shivered across the steps. The young man leapt to its defence, apologising to a lady seated in the first row as he steadied the candles.

He skipped up the steps and circled the dais, taper in hand and lit the footlights. Flames sputtered along the edge of the platform.

Metal scaffolding dominated the platform. Polished gears and brass pistons gleamed. Articulated rods reached down toward a large veiled box and disappeared under the drapery. Gold flecks glittered through the fine-gauzed linen.

Viola adjusted her eyepatch and bit her lip. She turned to her companion.

"Henry! How exciting."

Henry patted her hand and smiled. "I thought you might be intrigued."

She gripped his hand. "Who wouldn't?"

She turned to the sarcophagus and licked her lips.

A real mummy!

"The mechanicals must have cost a fortune. The permits alone for such an ostentatious display would've cost several month's wages."

"They enjoy Royal favour," said Henry. "Mechanicals always help when trying to impress."

"Perhaps they need more patronage to pay off the spectacle?" whispered Viola.

She surveyed the sea of top hats, silk bonnets and perfect coiffures. Much of high society had responded to the invitation. Lady Calthorpe, always present at any notable function, sat a few rows in front. She fussed with her bag, glanced around and slipped on her spectacles.

A small group of scholarly looking gentleman stood near a candelabra, engaged in intense debate. Sir Archibald Huntington-Smythe, Doctor and specialist in biometric mechanical technology, peered back through the crowd. He dipped his hat in her direction and smiled. Viola nodded back.

"Henry, Sir Archibald's here."

"Hardly surprising. He designed the mechanicals," replied Henry.

"It would seem everyone who's anyone is here tonight."

Clouds of steam hissed and puffed into the air and rolled along the ceiling.

The audience gasped.

More candles flickered to life behind the contraption, revealing a towering statue, half hawk-half man, staring back through the forest of candelabra.

The audience hushed.

Viola's eye widened and fixed on the veiled sarcophagus before them.

A lanky, beak-nosed gentleman emerged from behind one of the curtains on the dais. His hand slid along the crest of the sarcophagus, pausing to rest at the foot. He straightened his shoulders and beamed at the seated aristocracy, scientists and assembled society.

"Good evening, gentlemen." His voice boomed over their heads. "And ladies. My name is Mr Chartha, assistant to our esteemed head of Egyptian Antiquities, Professor Fosse." Chartha bowed low, not taking his eyes off his audience. He cleared his throat. "I'm afraid Professor Fosse has been unavoidably detained. However, the British Museum welcomes you. Tonight we celebrate our latest acquisition from the tombs of Egypt with the unwrapping of the mummy."

Another murmur rolled through the audience. Chartha raised his hands.

"Never fear, the unwrapping will continue on schedule and I will be able to answer any and all questions."

He clapped his hands together. "Now, shall we start?" His gaze flickered over the veiled sarcophagus entombed within the scaffold. "Here we have an untouched mummy from the nineteenth dynasty. The markings confirm it is a royal sarcophagus - a princess. Possibly a queen. Queen Mehytenweskhet?" He grinned at the audience as his tongue rolled effortlessly over the word. "So, we are anticipating some valuable treasures to be encased within the linen wrappings.”

All you need now is a basket and a snake.

Chantha reached down beside the coffin and pulled a lever on the scaffolding. The contraption chugged into life.

The crowd gasped.

“Who among you is brave enough to join me in removing the initial wrappings?” Mr Chartha grabbed the edge of the linen and flicked it off the sarcophagus.

The woman shrieked in the chair beside Viola.

Viola winced and shook her head, her ears still ringing as the woman slumped. Her husband slipped his arm around her waist and fanned her furiously.

Viola rubbed her ear. *Such a commotion over nothing.*

Chartha pointed in their direction. “You sir, would you like the honour?”

Viola gasped. *A chance to unwrap a mummy!*

Henry shook his head. A tinge of red crept along his earlobe.

“It seems the gentleman needs some encouragement. Mr Turner, would you escort the gentleman.”

Viola smiled. “Go on, Henry. It sounds like fun.”

Henry nudged Viola. He lifted her hand into the air, enticing her to her feet.

“But Henry, you –”

A familiar voice spoke by her ear. “Go on, Doctor Stewart,” said Sir Archibald. “I unwrapped my first mummy at the London Museum. It’s a curious thing, not unlike an autopsy.”

Henry took her hand in his. “You go, Viola.” He nudged her towards Turner, who now stood at the end of their row. “It’ll give you something to tell Doyle next time you visit.”

“Sir?” Turner held out his arm toward the dais.

“Go, Viola. Since when have you been so shy?” said Sir Archibald.

~ VIII ~

Viola pulled in her skirts and edged past Henry. A frown flickered over Turner's forehead.

The woman next to Viola roused. Her hands trembled. "But the curse... ?"

Read the entire story in

Eye of the Beholder & Other Tales: The Adventures of Viola Stewart Journal #2

Mummies.
Murder.
Madness.

~ X ~

~ X ~